THE NEW BADGE

ISBN: 978-0-9829756-5-7
Published by:
First School Press
P.O. Box 115
Sodus, Michigan 49126

Edited by Rachel Starr Thomson
Cover Design by Jay Cookingham
Kindle Formatting by Carolyn Currey

Printed in the United States of America

THE NEW BADGE

MICHAEL LEONARD JEWELL

Dedication

To my brothers: Lt. Daniel Burton Jewell,
Berrien County Sheriff's Dept., and Deputy John Rice
Jewell,
Berrien County Sheriff's Tether Dept.

To David Agens, Undersheriff (retired), Berrien County
Sheriff's Dept.,
currently the director, Berrien County Dispatch Center.
Thanks, Boss, for all of your patience through the years.

In memory of my friend Deputy Michael P. Moore,
Badge#271,
Berrien County Sheriff's Dept.
Your final call for service went unanswered on October 17,
2012.

Robert Chandler Oakes (Lane Chandler),
June 4, 1899—September 14, 1972
Cowboy and film star, born on a horse ranch
near Culbertson, Montana.
(*Winds of the Wasteland* with John Wayne, 1936)

Table of Contents

Prologue
PRAIRIE MARSHAL

Pete Randers sat thoughtfully at his desk in the lonely quiet of the jail house, fingering his new marshal's badge that was pinned just above his heart. It was shiny and new with no scratches or dings, unlike his old deputy's badge he had worn for years while working for crusty old Marshal Brenton who had retired to Oregon with his wife Melinda. The old marshal had recommended Pete take his place, and now that the job was his, he was the only lawman in north-central Montana and the town of Cantana. With no deputy hired to assist him, he would have to go it alone for the time being.

Standing up to pour himself a coffee, Pete's attention was drawn to a shiny brown belt and holster with the butt end of a large caliber revolver sticking out, folded neatly and laying on a shelf against the wall behind his desk. Pete reached out and touched it, smiling to himself as he remembered the mounted policeman, Sergeant Jim LaForge, who had worn it. He had left instructions for Pete

1

to give it to his son, Daniel, on his next journey to town.

Jim LaForge had been a friend and frequent visitor to Cantana from above the border for many years but had put away his red serge coat after a long and distinguished career with the North-West Mounted Police. He and his wife Marta had also set out west to Oregon with the Brentons to retire and fulfill a desire to see more of the United States, leaving behind as part of their legacy to Canada their only son, Corporal Daniel LaForge.

Pete remembered the day when he held his hat high, standing by the edge of the tracks to see them all off from the Havre station. As the train and the smoke from its stack disappeared into a black dot in the distance, he felt the heaviness inside as the responsibility of office subtly shifted to himself. He would want God's wisdom for sure.

Pete had been courting the schoolteacher, Alice Granfield, who lived with her adopted parents at the hotel they owned. Granfield House, as it was called, was the only establishment in town where a person might get a bath, a clean bed, and a decent sit-down supper with linen tablecloths.

Alice loved Pete intensely even though she was in many ways his opposite. Formally educated and versed in all the social graces, she was very much at home among a room full of swells. Even so, she was content in her day-in and day-out existence among the rough cowboys, common citizens, and transient visitors to the Montana prairie and seemed never to weary of them. She had made the prairie her home and was happy living in Cantana. She knew what she wanted. Pete loved and admired her for that, and although he had not formally asked her to marry him, they had a clear understanding.

Pete often thought about his two friends, Arliss Moore and Tom Brumett, with whom he had shared the greatest adventure of his life. Arliss was a retired buffalo soldier from nearby Fort Assiniboine and had been temporarily reinstated in the cavalry to escort the remnants of Chief Michael's band of Nez Perce Indians to the Colville Reservation in Washington State. Pete had not heard from him since that day they were parted at Fort Assiniboine. He thought perhaps that Arliss had made a decision to remain with the army or return home to his folks in Texas. Pete didn't really expect to ever see him again, but he would miss him. Arliss Moore was the only black man Pete had ever been close to, and he believed that had Arliss lived in another time and place, he would have been recognized and honored for the remarkable man that he was.

Tom Brumett, the young doctor's son from Idaho, now a lieutenant at Fort Assiniboine, was earning his credentials as a medical doctor. During his part in the adventure to rescue the missionaries hiding in the Bear Paw Mountains, he had developed a serious fondness for their lovely young daughter, Judith Farnsworth. It was generally thought they would be getting together, but when the mission to the Bear

3

Paws was over, he had kissed her hand as she boarded the train going east and that was that. With her parents slain and the Nez Perce safely at Colville, her ministry days were over for the present, and she had decided to accept the invitation from her wealthy aunt and uncle in Chicago to go live with them, perhaps to get an education and some refinement and decide what her future should be.

Pete continued to worry about the fate of Cantana, a town seemingly disconnected from the rest of Montana. If the railroad would only make good its promise to lay a new spur north to the border and repair the telegraph lines, Cantana could be easily supplied, attracting new businesses and residents and encouraging its prosperity. But if not, the town would expire and be left a ruin of decaying old buildings on a featureless prairie—a monument to the failed hopes and dreams of those who dared to come and build here. Whatever Cantana had become or would become, it was now Pete's life and his home.

As the 1890s pressed to a close, Cantana stood at the doorstep of a new century. Pete could not have imagined in his job as a Montana lawman the events that would draw him out and stretch him as much or even more than his journey to the Bear Paw Mountains.

1
SUMMER SNOW

Pete was returning to Cantana one late afternoon from a long ride to one of the outlying ranches, investigating a report of cattle rustling. As he rode into town, dusty and weary, Pete stopped at Bill Hester's livery to feed and water his horse Sadie. As he figured, there was work waiting for him and in a few hours, he would have to head back out to serve some papers in the town of Hogeland as a courtesy for the county sheriff. But to his chagrin, the air had suddenly turned chilly and overnight, an angry freak snowstorm raged along the border with Canada.

Snowbound early for the first time in several years by what Pete referred to as a summer snow, he was forced to wait it out, hoping that it would soon melt and give them a beautiful Indian summer before the long winter had a chance to formally sink its frosty teeth deep into the prairie sod.

Unlike previous years, there would be plenty of supplies to go around—mostly a credit to Pete for using his newfound authority as marshal to twist the arms of errant suppliers. Sending out a barrage of letters on the town's letterhead to purveyors in Chinook and Havre and other places along the tracks of the Hi-line, he had reminded them that Cantana's winter orders of dry goods, coal, and kerosene must be delivered no later than the last week of August. Curtly stating the facts, he made it clear that late deliveries or no deliveries at all would not be tolerated. Thanks to the quartermaster at Fort Assiniboine, an old friend of Pete's father, the merchants were encouraged to be more diligent as the army hinted that it would not look kindly or do business with anyone who would neglectfully allow the citizens of Cantana to suffer and starve.

There were grumblings, of course, and Pete was aware of what some of the merchants in Havre were saying behind his back and even to his face, that he was just a young upstart hiding behind the authority of his new badge, enlisting the help of his father's friends in a pathetic attempt to fill the larger boots of his old boss. But Pete had known heroes and cowards all his life, and the heroes were just the ones who, when facing adversity, just seemed to get things done anyhow. He reasoned that there being no mayor in Cantana, it was his responsibility as the town's only appointed official to do what he could to help.

Pete was thoughtful and circumspect about his role as the new marshal, just as anyone might be who had been given some real authority for the first time. Should he flex his muscles and burst out of the bullpen with his guns blazing, be his own man, and show everyone that he had what it took, or ease into the job by following in his predecessor's way of taking it as it came?

Marshal Brenton and his dear wife were sincerely loved and missed by everyone. They had been a team, making the challenge of any given situation sometimes appear almost effortless to overcome. Pete had wanted to be marshal for a long time, but even after years learning at the feet of the old marshal, he wasn't exactly sure of the elements that made it work. He would try to remember that Cantana was a small town, and as much as possible, seek a balance between his style and that of his old mentor.

Pete had been preoccupied for most of the summer with the task of hiring a new deputy. If his work never drew him farther than the borders of the town he could handle it by himself, but because of the remoteness of Cantana and the county seat being so far away, he had been deputized by the sheriff at Fort Benton, giving him far-reaching authority throughout the vast county of Choteau. This sometimes expanded his work and business to the outlying ranches and small towns and frequently to the Hi-line. Also, he was sometimes prevailed upon to assist the Mounties with an arrest along the Canadian border, which was visible on a clear day just north of town. So to do the job right, he needed a second man.

Alice had helped him by placing advertisements with

various newspapers, post offices, and train depots along the Hi-line from glacier country in the west to Culbertson near the North Dakota border. She was motivated and understood that the sooner Pete was able to hire that all important number two man, they would be able to set a definite date for a wedding. But several men had applied as a result, but none of them seemed right for the job.

One man from Wyoming who had worked twelve years as a bounty hunter seemed experienced enough, but he was cold and aloof, never smiling, and Pete sensed a mean streak in him. He soon sent the man packing, not willing to hire a deputy who might go about bullying the town folk and finding trouble where there was none. Pete and Marshal Brenton had never been particularly fond of bounty hunters, deeming them to be illegitimate lawmen who only regarded their badges as tools and toys to allow them to catch men for profit.

Another young aspirant, untried but hopeful, had ridden in from Turner. Pete sensed the young ranch hand's inexperience and timidity, doubting whether he would be able to back him when needed or stand up to a tough cowpoke who had too much to drink. Unsure if the kid was just shy or a genuine coward, Pete decided to settle the matter by pulling an unloaded revolver from his desk, pointing it at the kid's nose, and pulling the trigger.

The metallic drop of the hammer caused the young man's eyes to bug out as he fell backwards out of his chair.

Picking up his hat and dashing out the door of the marshal's office, he mounted his horse and rode away pronto, back to the tiny burg of Turner and the quieter existence to which he was accustomed.

A few years in the cavalry might put some spine in 'im, Pete thought with a quick shake of his head.

Pete took no pleasure in humiliating the boy but perhaps the little experiment had been good for them both. The young man learned some things about himself that he wouldn't have understood any other way, and Pete was reminded again that the job was indeed a serious one.

Marshal Brenton had taught him that unorthodox methods were sometimes called for. Pete would never forget the kangaroo court set up by the marshal and the old judge to save his friend Tom Brumett from the hanging tree. He too would be willing to try almost anything as long as it was for the greater good and fair in the end.

2
CORPORAL LaFORGE

Corporal Daniel LaForge had not been near the border of the United States for many months. Constrained to work near his home base in Regina, he had been prevailed upon to work at the Old Depot with the training of new recruits. But today, he was headed west again on a mission, accompanied by two other NWMP constables, having received word that a suspicious death had occurred in a small settlement known as Val Marie just north of the Montana border. The sparsely populated town was mostly French but fortunately, he and one of the other officers spoke it fluently. They were directed to investigate, make a report and bring the suspect in for trial with any witnesses. But right after the investigation, Corporal Dan would part ways with his two partners and head south on another assignment of his own.

* * *

After months of duty at headquarters, rubbing elbows with

fellow officers and new recruits, enjoying a somewhat unaccustomed social life, he was soon off again by himself, doing what he liked, spending his days on horseback and his nights camping out on the prairie grass.

His work along the United States border necessarily brought LaForge in contact with American law enforcement and the US Army, dealing with miscreants that often were not aware of the international line or just didn't care. It was only natural on the loneliness of the prairie that friendships might be struck between Mounties and marshals of small towns along the border as kindred spirits enforcing the law. It had been so with Dan's father, Sergeant Jim LaForge, and Marshal Brenton, and it was no surprise that Dan and Marshal Pete had become close friends. But unlike his father, Dan did not have a wife or devoted girlfriend waiting for him back home in Regina or Toronto.

So for a young Mountie accustomed to batching it at a wilderness log cabin outpost in the territory or setting up a meager camp along a narrow stream, it was almost heaven to enjoy, now and then, a tasty supper with trusted friends and a night's sleep under clean sheets at Granfield House. And so, a gentle pull on the reins and Daniel LaForge was again headed south across the invisible Medicine Line to Cantana, this time with the excuse of being on official business for the Queen.

* * *

The clouded August sky in the northwest was gray and dark, and the distant rumblings of thunder announced an approaching storm. The tall yellow grasses were soon thrashing to and fro by swirling winds as if trod upon by the feet of an invisible giant, lumbering along in the wake of his fury. Soon the raindrops fell, hard at first, then moderating into a fine steady drizzle. But Pete didn't care. The wet would settle the dust on the streets and hopefully dampen and quell the desire for mischief among the dozen or so cowboys who had just ridden into town. They were tired and thirsty and headed directly to the Red Angus saloon at the end of the street.

The Red Angus was owned by an immigrant cattleman from Scotland, Jack Macgregor, who had brought a herd of red Angus cattle to the Montana prairie with aspirations of establishing a herd of these beautiful animals. However, tragedy struck when he was frozen out during the terrible snows of the 1880s, and taking what money he had left, Jack came to Cantana to find a place for himself as a merchant selling and dispensing spirits.

A quiet place, the Red Angus was not usually troublesome. Macgregor made everyone check their guns at the bar, and he was not above breaking a bottle over the head of an unruly ranch hand. Yet, a weary cowboy might get himself something cool to drink and a tasty bowl of hot stew or chili and a generous slice of cornbread or a sourdough biscuit if he behaved himself.

It was late afternoon, and Pete decided to go to supper at Granfield House and spend some time with Alice before returning to the marshal's office to be close by in case the drinking at the saloon got out of hand. He knew that Alice was anxious to get married, but until he could hire a competent deputy to share the work, he didn't see how he could set a date. So Pete had resigned himself to living in the jail, spending his quiet evenings walking the dark streets and alleys of Cantana, and making a presence at the Red Angus.

Locking the door to his office, Pete pulled the brim of his hat down and his collar up to prevent rain from dripping down the back of his neck. Stepping off the boardwalk headed to Granfield House, he could hear a snort and whinny and the clomping of horse hooves further up the street. Pete turned to see the flash of a red serge jacket beneath a black rain slicker worn by Corporal Dan LaForge of the North-West Mounted Police.

Pete had first met Dan when as a young man he came to visit with his father. Dan was born and had spent all of his youth in Regina with his mother, but when older, he was allowed to shadow his father as he performed his duties throughout the southern part of the territory. Dan had realized early on that he wanted to follow in his father's footsteps, and now that he was a proper man and had finished his training at the Old Depot in Regina, he was a seasoned Mountie in his own right. Thanks to the workings of a somewhat nostalgic superintendant, he had been assigned to his father's old jurisdiction, bringing him frequently close to the Montana border.

"Ho, Danny!" Pete exclaimed, happy to see his young friend.

Corporal LaForge reached down and shook hands with Pete. "Can you put up a vagabond for a while?" he asked. "I'm on crown business this trip, and your army from the fort is to be meeting me here with a prisoner going back to Regina for trial. Until then, I am to stay put and enjoy your American hospitality."

"You're always welcome, of course," Pete responded. "Let's take care of your horse and then head over to Granfield House and get you a room. It's roast grouse, creamed onions, and those little potatoes for supper, Alice tells me. She and her folks will be glad to hear any news you might have. Canadian gossip is just as good as American when you're starved for news."

* * *

Soon after Corporal Dan's arrival, a fast rider from Fort Assiniboine had brought news of the impending visit by the army with a prisoner for extradition back to Canada. A detail of troopers from Fort Assiniboine was expected to arrive in two days' time and they'd requested to have their meal at Granfield House, causing everyone to scurry about to make ready for their accommodation. Visits like these from the army were rare these days but welcome as they paid well, and Granfield House could certainly use the added revenue.

Early morning of the expected day, Alice carried a heavy bushel of potatoes, carrots, and onions up the stairs from the cool root cellar to the kitchen. Setting it down with a thump, she wiped her forehead with the towel draped across her shoulder. Isabelle, the Cree woman who ran the kitchen, was diligently slicing off chunks of meat from the quarter of beef Mr. Granfield had hung from the hook in the corner.

As late afternoon approached, the detail of soldiers could be seen coming from the southwest, the flag from their guidon blowing in the wind. Three of the men—a lieutenant and a private leading a beshackled prisoner on horseback—broke ranks and rode ahead to the marshal's office to make arrangements for the lodging of their man. Soon, the prisoner was locked safely in his cell and a guard posted by the army until Corporal LaForge could officially accept him into custody. The lieutenant and the remainder of his men made their way to Granfield House for supper and some rest.

* * *

After a fine meal of roasted beef, glazed carrots and onions, mushrooms, garlic mashed potatoes, and white cake for dessert, the men cheerfully repaired to the sitting room to talk. A young lieutenant lighting a cheroot cigar approached Pete where he stood by the window.

"Marshal Randers? I have a letter here for you, compliments of an old friend, Captain Brumett," he said, handing him a sealed envelope from his pocket.

Pete smiled, accepting the envelope. "Yes, we are good friends. I hadn't heard of his promotion to captain."

"Well, in times of war," the young officer said. "Promotions sometimes come swiftly. Before leaving Fort Assiniboine months ago, Captain Brumett asked that I find you and give you this letter. I'm sorry I was only now able to get it to you."

Pete immediately begged the officer's pardon and hasted to leave the room, and finding a bright table lamp, he opened the envelope and began to read:

Dear Marshal Peter Randers,

It's been a long time since we have spoken, and our adventure to the mountains seems a decade ago. You might have heard they made my father's son a captain, and now I have men working under me. How things have changed from that day I felt the noose tightening about my throat.

I want to bring you up to date on what is happening here with me. My original plans were

16

to get out of the army as soon as I could, and
either return to Idaho to help my father or
move to Cantana and be your doctor there. You
know I was sort of sweet on Judith Farnsworth
and had written her several times, but her
letters seemed to come fewer and fewer apart
and finally stopped altogether. I guess I can
take a hint. Living the life of a wealthy
debutant in Chicago has got to beat out the
poverty of an officer's wife in Indian country.
I have quit my dreaming and as fate would have
it, I've met someone here at the fort, the
lovely daughter of a colonel. We were married a
month ago, and I hope for you to meet her
sometime.

What I really needed to tell you is that I
have received orders to ship out to Cuba. As you
know, we are at war with Spain, and President
McKinley has ordered up troops. They're going
to need doctors in Cuba and in the Philippines,
so I don't know when or if I'll ever see you
again. Whatever happens, I wanted you to know
that we are brothers and that I can never
forget what you and Marshal Brenton did for
me. I also want to thank that judge for not
hanging me. Ha!

P.S. If you ever get to see that big buffalo
soldier again, tell him I miss him and that he
is my big brother too. Tell him I'll think about
him in Cuba and that I'm proud to serve with
these guys of the 10th.

Thomas Evans Brumett,

Tom

Captain and Surgeon, 10th Cavalry.

Pete folded the letter and stuffed it back into its envelope. Walking across the veranda of Granfield House, he made his way south of town through the grass until Cantana was but a cluster of buildings on the horizon behind him. He needed to be alone, to think about Tom and Arliss and what they had been through together and what their friendship would always mean.

My soul! Cuba and the Philippines? he thought. *It wasn't that long ago they wanted to hang Tom on a mistaken charge of horse theft on the Montana frontier, and now he's a doctor and will be caring for bloodied men fighting a war with Spain.*

Pete bowed his head. *Dear Lord Jesus, please be with Tom and keep him safe. Whatever may befall him, bring him back to us and his wife safely, I pray.*

3
A LAWMAN COMES TO SUPPER

One dark night Pete arrested a man in the Red Angus for fighting and shooting up the place, later discovering the man had a wanted poster for theft out of Chinook. Since the only communication with the marshal in Chinook was by mail, Pete decided to save time and take the prisoner there himself.

After a long ride, Pete arrived at the Chinook jail late in the afternoon of the following day, and anxious to get headed back north to Cantana, he declined an offer to spend the night even though the marshal had offered him a clean bunk and blanket.

As he was about to leave town, a man approached him out of the shadows, holding one of the handbills advertising the job of deputy marshal for Cantana. Pete quickly agreed to sit down with him to talk in a nearby eatery over a cup of coffee.

"Name's Ronald Guidice," he began with a bold, haughty smile and laugh. "I pronounce it 'Judas' just like the wayward apostle in the Bible." Pete listened patiently as the man went on about his several years spent in the cavalry as an Indian fighter and his time as a deputy sheriff further south in New Mexico. There was no doubt that he sounded experienced, but the more he prattled on, the more Pete took a disliking to him. He was a cocky braggart and a bit of a dandy, having more silver trimmings on his vest, gun belt, and boots than at the Carson City Mint.

If he was a cat he'd lick himself and purr, Pete thought, detecting a dark undercurrent in the man that was difficult to explain. He had a sense of humor, but there was something about his insincere painted-on smile and gray, motionless, half-opened eyes that smacked of cruelty.

Guidice chuckled out loud when Pete told him he couldn't use him, but it was evident that gears were turning in the man's head, and he wasn't happy being turned down.

As Pete mounted his faithful horse, Sadie, to ride out of town, he glanced behind him. The strange man just stood there smiling, his hands on his gun belt, watching him as he made his way up the street. Pete could feel the hairs stiffen on his neck as he imagined the man's dead, dreamy eyes fixed upon him as he rode out of sight.

Nudging Sadie slightly to hurry her on, he was glad to be headed home, hoping he had seen the last of this stranger. The man probably thought Pete the prince of all idiots for allowing such a fine, experienced lawman as Ronald Guidice slip through his fingers. But Pete also wondered about himself . . . if perhaps he was being too fussy, holding these prospective men to a near impossible standard. And was he unconsciously dragging his feet to delay his marriage to Alice?

* * *

Pete followed the meager path out of town for about two hours until it faded into the thick prairie grass. As he made his way through a coulee with long shadows, the rising chill in the   low places gripped him about the neck and shoulders and caused him to shiver.

As the sun finally slipped below the western horizon with a fiery wink, Pete had located a spot with a pool of fresh water that Sadie could drink. Dismounting, he quickly dug around in his baggage for his cup and coffeepot, and setting up the folding cook rack that Bill Hester the blacksmith had made for him several years ago, he cleared off a spot sheltered from the wind to build his fire. Setting the pot to boil, he unrolled his bedding on a dry patch downwind of the fire's heat. Finally, with Sadie fed and watered, Pete settled back against his saddle with his steaming cup, listening to the haunting silence.

Then, somewhere in the distance, he could hear the unnerving sound of a rabbit being methodically torn to bits by a coyote. Pete could almost feel the terror in the small creature's fast-beating heart, see the blood and tufts of fur scattering in the wind. The sound was almost human, like the cry of a baby or a small child, shattering the solemnity of the place. Finally it was over, and Pete was glad.

Always impressed by how quickly the prairie could get dark and quiet under a moonless sky, Pete stared off into the ink of the night and was therefore surprised when he thought he saw a flash of light in the distance. Continuing to watch, he saw the flicker several more times, perhaps several hundred yards away. Quickly packing up his belongings, he dumped the contents of his coffeepot over the fire and kicked the remnants out across the grass. Carefully leading Sadie along the coulee to investigate, Pete was startled when there before him was a door that seemed to open up in the side of a hill, blazing with light. It was apparently a sod house built in the middle of this sea of grass.

As Pete cautiously approached the spot, he heard the unmistakable cocking of hammers from a double-barreled shotgun.

"Now that's far enough, fella," a deep, low voice with an eastern twang rang out from the dark. "Up with the hands and show yourself against the light."

Pete complied. What choice did he have? He could be shot and buried out here and no one would know the better. Turning slowly on his heels, he held his hands high, palms forward.

"Now state your business. What's with this nightprowlin' about?" the voice queried.

Pete swallowed hard. "Can I open my coat?" he asked.

"Go ahead," said the voice from shadows, "but I'll blast ya if you try anything."

Pete reached down and pulled back the front of his coat, catching the light from the open door against the shine of his badge. "I'm Pete Randers, marshal up north in Cantana by the border. I was in Chinook delivering them a prisoner; didn't know there was anyone living out here."

If this citizen doesn't respect the law, I'm still in a heap of trouble, he thought, wondering if the man would show himself or if he would only see the momentary muzzle flash of the shotgun before it cut him in half.

The silence seemed long as Pete waited to find out if the man was true or just a saddle bum hiding from the law. He heard some rustling and then a tall man stepped from the darkness holding a double-barreled ten-gauge Greener shotgun almost identical to his own. The man looked to be about Pete's age and stood over six feet tall. One pant leg was tucked into his boot and the other hung out. His suspenders dangling from his waist indicating that he had scrambled to deal with the intruder outside.

The man approached Pete with the barrels of his shotgun still pointed at his middle until he was well satisfied of the lawman's identity. "Marshal of Cantana, huh? I always wondered about that place. Heard it was mighty quiet—almost dead. Well, you can put your hands down and tie your horse under the overhang there.

"Peg?" he shouted over his shoulder into the darkness behind him. "Reheat the coffee and the stew. It's a lawman come to supper." Pointing his shotgun toward the ground this time and slowly releasing the cocked hammers, the man stepped forward, holding his hand out for a shake. "By the way—name's Ben Hamilton."

* * *

The one-roomed soddy was warm and tight, muffling the sounds of the September wind as it rose and moved through the prairie grasses, intensifying the closeness of the small room. It was a strange but not unfamiliar experience—cozy and hospitable, but wild and primitive at the same time. The smell of antelope stew flavored with Pete's offering of smoky bacon and a sprig of wild sage, mixed with the earthy, damp smell of the walls and floor, made his stomach rumble with hunger. Mrs. Hamilton's freshly baked sourdough bread, leavened with wild yeast from scrapings of aspen bark, was beyond tasty when used to sop up the rich brown gravy of the stew.

Pete took another sip of his coffee. "This here is some fine victuals, Mrs. Hamilton. I thank you again for your hospitality."

"You are welcome, Marshal. It's pleasing to have some company. Ben and I have been out here since a year ago spring. We built this soddy to get through the winter while trying to find our way as to what we want to do, and we are still here. I was a schoolmarm back east in Indiana, and my husband, Ben here, was a policeman."

Pete's ears perked up. "Policeman? What made you come out here to the wilderness? Lookin' for gold or wanting to start a ranch?"

"Something the likes of that," Ben answered with a soft chuckle. "Peg and I are still young enough and thought we could see what the rest of the country looked like. I didn't figure we'd end up living in a hole in the ground like two gophers. It's been an adventure, though."

"How long were you a policeman in Indiana, Ben?" Pete inquired.

"About five years. I was offered the position of chief when the old man retired, but Peg and I had already made our decision to come out west."

Pete held his coffee cup with both hands and stared into it. *Up until now, I've waited for the right man to come to me. Maybe I should change that and seek after the right man myself.*

Pete gulped another mouthful of coffee and spoke with resolve. "Ben, I don't know you and you don't know me, but I'm going to do something that I hope I'll never regret. How would you like to come work for me and be my deputy in Cantana? You and Mrs. Hamilton can move to town; I even have a place where you can live. You're a lawman—not a farmer. You can try it for a while, and if it doesn't suit you, there'll be no hard feelings. Just say the word and we can pack you up and head north in the morning. There are some mighty fine folks living in Cantana."

Peg Hamilton looked at her husband, her eyes growing large as she carelessly knocked over a bag of table salt. It was clear that she was troubled by the suddenness of the offer.

"Marshal, I don't mean to get involved in menfolk's talk, and it is a fine, generous proposal, and I'm grateful, but I just can't turn the corner that quickly in my head. Ben and I need time to talk it over, perhaps a long time. We were thinking of getting some cows and chickens and planting a large garden. And . . . I'm expecting." Peg blushed, instinctively putting her hands on her waist. "Can you give us time to think about it?"

Ben smiled and took another sip of his coffee. "Sorry, Marshal. Peg here is a schoolteacher used to dealing with tough Hoosier farm boys. She's not shy and speaks her mind."

Pete gave his head a quick shake. "What a dunderhead I am. Of course you will need time to think about it. I will be leaving early in the morning, but before I go, I'll make you a map to Cantana should you decide to come. There'll be no ill will if you should think better of the idea. I'll even leave you my old compass just to show you I'm serious about my offer. Cantana is a speck on the Canadian border—easy to miss if you're not used to looking for it. If I don't hear from you in a week or two, I'll figure you decided against it. You can send the compass back to me in the mail; mark it 'Town Marshal, Cantana, Montana' when you can."

Peg reached out and took Pete's empty cup. "Marshal, I didn't mean to be impertinent."

Pete smiled as he spoke. "Menfolk are sometimes abrupt and don't consider their women when making plans, but let me say, we have cows and chickens and some mighty fine gardens and places to live in Cantana. And it might be a comfort to know that we have some pretty clever women who can help when your time comes."

Pete checked on Sadie one last time and then spread his bedroll on the floor before the stove as the Hamilton's turned down the lantern. He was regretful to have upset Mrs. Hamilton. *Anyway, if Ben wanted to be a lawman, he would have stayed in Indiana and taken that promotion as chief of police,* he thought as he drifted off to sleep to the sound of the wind in the grass.

4
ARLISS MOORE

"Let's go, you old nail bender—ain't got all day!" barked the tall dusty cowboy, his feet propped against the massive anvil of Bill Hester's blacksmith and livery. He lazily chewed his cud of tobacco, the resulting dark ooze draining through his clenched brown teeth into his stubble. "You said you'd have those horses shod by midmornin' and here it's past the midday!"

The man's partner, standing nearby, walked over and stood at Hester's side. "Looks here like Grand pappy shoulda put out to pasture years ago," he growled as he repeatedly struck a short-handled whip known as a quirt against his leather chaps to intimidate the aging blacksmith. As Bill Hester struggled to pull bits of old nail from the horse's hoof, the bully proceeded to strike his whip harder and faster in anger, shouting in the old blacksmith's ear, "The ramrod's gonna give us holy Hades for gettin' back so late, and it's your doin'!"

Bill Hester had turned seventy-five last month and had owned the blacksmith shop and livery business in Cantana since the town was first platted years ago. A younger man in those days, he was full of vigor and ideas of making a good living caring for all the horses that would be coming through with the cattle drives and from nearby ranches. He would never have stood for this kind of abuse back then, but now he was an old man suffering from what must have been a mild stroke, leaving his right arm weak and his hammer hand and fingers without their former cunning. So now he must allow himself to be put upon and forced into the humility of keeping his mouth shut.

"Jis be patient, gentlemen. Ain't what I used ta be; got a little behind this mornin'," Bill said. His face was dripping with perspiration and smeared with ash from the hot forge. He was physically agitated and almost out of breath but helpless to do anything about it.

The first cowboy stood up and hovered menacingly over Bill. "You kept us waitin' old man, so I know yer not expectin' to be paid." The foulness of the man intensified when he spat into the glowing bed of hot coals, the ensuing puff of acrid steam sizzling and dancing over the forge like a tiny hellish imp. Wiping his mouth with his hand, the cowboy purposely stood in range of the old man's elbow, making it difficult for him to work without bumping his tormentor's gun belt. Smoke and heat stung Bill's eyes as the pungent odor of a week's worth of body odor, tobacco dribble, and cow manure turned his stomach.

Bill Hester's fingers began to quiver and tremble like

the nervous forelegs of an insect, causing him to drop his pliers in the loose slag beneath the forge, and as he bent over to retrieve them, a shadow darkened the doorway to the livery as if a cloud had passed against the sun.

"Seems to me the old man would do a whole lot better without you boys hanging over him," a deep voice rang out.

The two cowboys turned to look behind them, letting their hands slide to their holsters. Standing there, holding the reins of his horse was Arliss Moore, the former buffalo soldier. The cowboys slowly pulled their hands away from their guns as they silently looked the giant of a man up and down.

"I've been around horseflesh all my life, and I set great store by the men that take care of them. And if by chance your hoo-rawin' about should cause this man here to quick-nail that horse," Arliss said sternly, "I'll most likely have to shoot one of you in the foot—just to give you the idea of how it feels."

The two cowboys did not know what to make of this man who stood by his horse confidently staring holes through them to show that he was not intimidated, letting his gun hand dangle. The men chose to remain still, careful not to make any threatening gestures by slowly withdrawing their hands to perch on their gun belts.

"Now, why don't you boys go after your dinner, and when you come back, your horses will be shod." Arliss smiled at the two cowboys as he tied his horse at the nearby rail. "And remember, don't spend all of your money. I'm sure you'll be wantin' to pay the man here what you owe him."

Nodding at Bill Hester, Arliss stooped to pick up the fallen tool and proceeded to finish shoeing the horse. With a perplexed look, Bill mopped up the sweat from his face with his soiled neckerchief and seated himself in his old chair near the forge. The situation diffused for now, the two cowboys smirked and shrugged in an effort to hold on to their dignity, but then with certain uneasiness, they turned and walked together in the direction of the Red Angus saloon.

* * *

A large deck of white clouds were visible in the distance over the Canadian prairie as if someone had hung a pale curtain against the sky, the contrast between the white and blue fixed and sharp. But any potential storms that might come of it were yet many miles and many hours away. The few citizens of Cantana were accustomed to living with the impending weather as if it were the town's resident drunkard—usually of little concern but worth keeping an eye on.

Arliss had finished his shoeing of the horses belonging to the two ill-behaved cowboys, and they having paid their money to Bill with a gratuity besides were long on their way back to their ranch without further ado. In fact, with Arliss standing by, cooling his face in the horse trough with a wet neckerchief, the boys even managed a halfhearted apology, having thought the matter through should the ramrod or rancher find out they had been harassing the well-liked Bill Hester, the only blacksmith within thirty miles of Cantana.

Having been invited to supper by Bill, Arliss took the stout rake that was leaning against the wall and began to clean up the area around the forge to kill time. Hearing the subtle crunch of footsteps on the gravel behind him, Arliss wheeled about, and pausing, began to laugh out loud. He dropped his rake. Standing there with an ear-to-ear grin was Pete Randers, and the two men heartedly shook hands and slapped each other on the shoulder.

"I knew it had to be you when I heard it," Pete said. "I don't know too many men who could stare down the McGuffy brothers and get away with it. Were you really going to shoot 'em?"

"I don't know," Arliss answered, "but neither did they. I'm glad I didn't have to find out."

"Let's get out of this sun," Pete said as the two men found the wooden bench in the shade against the wall. "What took ya so long to get here, Arliss? I wasn't sure if I would ever see you again."

Arliss scratched behind his ear and removed his hat. "I

don't remember being invited," he said thoughtfully.

Pete stared at the horizon, turning his hat in his hands. "I'm sorry about that, my friend, but I thought you understood you were welcome here. I hoped one day you'd find your way to Cantana. I even thought of asking you to be my deputy. I just offered the job to another fellow but don't know if he will take it; should know in a week or two. If he doesn't want it, I'd like you to have the job."

Arliss dug his heels into the soft earth beneath the bench. "Pete," he said with a grin, "you got enough troubles without taking on a black man to be your deputy. I know what I'm talking about. The time will come when I will have to handle some rough hand with a little too much drink in him, and one sight of me will change matters. A deputy marshal wearing a shiny tin badge trying to enforce the law will suddenly become a black man trying to be *uppity*."

"But Arliss . . ."

"No, Pete," Arliss said, holding his hand up. "I'm not interested. Too independent, and besides, I have something else in mind. But I would like to settle down here just to see what's open, if that's all right?"

"You are always welcome here as long as you'd like to stay. You and Tom Brumett are the closest thing I have to brothers. I'll never forget our adventure to the Bear Paws and what we went through together," Pete answered soberly.

"Tom Brumett?" Arliss responded. "How is that skinny doctor doin' these days?"

"I got a letter from him a while back," Pete answered. "He mentioned you in it. They promoted him to captain, and now he has several shavetail doctors working under him. It seems they have shipped him out to Cuba with your old unit the 10th Cavalry to fight the Spanish. I was hoping he would end up here to be our town doctor. Funny how things work."

"His cream rose quickly to the top of the milk can," Arliss remarked, picking up the rake again. "That boy's sharp."

Pete put on his hat. "Arliss, how does supper at Granfield House sound tonight? I'd like to introduce you to my girl, Alice."

"Could we make that tomorrow?" Arliss asked, pressing his hat on his head. "Bill Hester asked me to supper, and I have a few things I'd like to talk over with him. But I wouldn't mind coffee later this evening at your office."

"Very good; see you tonight then," Pete answered. The two men shook hands.

5
THE NEW DEPUTY

Pete's morning routine had begun as usual with the rekindling of the banked fire in the small cook stove. Adding water to dilute the pot of thick, cold coffee from the night before, Pete set out to shave and get dressed. He was surprised to hear a knock at the door of the marshal's office. This was early.

Pete quickly pulled on his pants and struggled with his boots. Another succession of knocks rang out, louder this time. "Hold on now! Don't be goin' hog wild!" Pete shouted, stomping his feet to secure his boots. "Did a flock of woodpeckers just light out on my door?"

Petulantly, Pete unlatched and quickly swung the heavy wooden door open to show his disdain for being bothered before the sun could rise. There, standing on the boardwalk in front of a loaded wagon, was Ben Hamilton from Indiana. His wife, Peggy, bundled up against the chill of the morning dew, sat in the wagon seat, grinning down at him and waving with a gloved hand.

"Sorry to irritate you, Marshal," Ben said. "Is that

deputy job still open?"

Reaching out to shake his hand, Pete grinned. "You better know it is. Let me help your good wife down from her perch." Reaching up, he took her hand and helped Peggy Hamilton to the boardwalk, all annoyance gone.

"Come on in, folks, out of this early chill. It's already snowing in the mountains, I'm sure. I'll have some coffee warmed up directly, and then we can have breakfast over at Granfield House. You never had better biscuits and gravy or eggs of a mornin' until you've had Isabelle's cookin'," Pete said.

Then looking over at Mrs. Hamilton with regret, he spoke softly. "Pardon, ma'am, meant no insult. I'll bet your breakfasts are a symphony for the tongue."

Peg chuckled at the marshal's attempt at eloquence and loosened her bonnet, letting it hang down the back of her neck. "There's no offense taken, Marshal. If you were a housewife, you would understand what a treat it is to have someone else do the cooking for a change. I can't wait to sample her fare. Is Isabelle your wife?"

"No, ma'am," Pete answered, shaking his head. "Isabelle is the cook at Granfield House. I'm not married, but Alice Granfield and I have a, well, an understanding."

Pete set two chairs in front of his desk and poured three cups of the reheated coffee. "It isn't much to brag about, but you certainly won't forget it either," Pete laughed. "Now let's get down to cases. Ben, I'm prepared to pay you seventy-five dollars a month. I wish I could pay you more, but there are other benefits. The marshal's office will furnish you with a horse and saddle. If you don't have your own hogleg, I have one here in the drawer that could stand some cleanin' if you don't mind a .44 Colt like mine, and all the ammunition you can carry. Have you folks any questions so far?"

Ben looked over at his wife, who sat expressionless, her eyes blinking. He had seen that look many times before back in Indiana when he left the house in the morning to go to work for the local police department. He reached over and squeezed her hand and smiled. She returned his smile and spoke under her breath. "It's okay, Ben."

Pete paused to give the couple a few moments, pretending he was looking through some papers from a stack on his desk. Then clearing the morning frog from his throat, Pete began again. "Um, also folks, I have a place for you to live. It's Marshal Brenton's old house just down the street. It's a nice, clean, and cozy place, ma'am, and I know you will like it. If all is agreeable, I'll take you down there after breakfast. Do you need some time to talk this over?"

The Hamilton's, still holding hands, looked at each other, smiling. "No, Marshal," Peg answered in her forward manner. "If Ben has no reservations, then neither do I."

Pete opened the center drawer before him and clutched the deputy's badge in his hand, the same badge he had worn for many years. Walking around the desk, he asked

Ben to stand up.

"Raise your right hand and repeat after me: 'I, Benjamin Hamilton, do solemnly swear to serve as deputy marshal for the Town of Cantana, County of Chouteau, State of Montana, and to discharge my office with honesty and integrity, and to enforce the laws under my jurisdiction faithfully.'"

"I will," Ben responded.

Pete centered and pinned the badge over Ben's left shirt pocket, just above his heart.

"Now, Deputy, you work for me. My first order for you is to follow me over to Granfield House for breakfast so I can introduce you folks to my girl, Alice."

6
JUDITH

It was nearly noon as Alice hurried down the boardwalk to the Hamilton's with a large hamper of food. Crossing dusty Main Street, she could see that Pete was already there, helping his newly hired deputy marshal move in and get settled. The Hamilton's had taken possession of Marshal Brenton's old home, which had been a dry goods store in days gone by. It was fairly roomy but cozy and lived in, large enough for a young married couple who might be expecting a baby.

Alice tapped on the door and was greeted by Peggy Hamilton, who had been dusting and wiping down the woodwork with a rag and a bucket of hot soapy water.

"I figured you would be busy today, so I thought it would be helpful if I brought over your dinner. There is plenty for everyone and enough leftovers for a supper if you wish," Alice said. She made no attempt to hide her delight that there would be another lady in town near her age, and also from the East.

"Thank you, Alice," Peggy said. "I think we are going

to be great friends."

Fortunately, the Brentons had left most of their larger pieces of furniture behind, so the house was well furnished, making the move a comfortable one.

"Peggy? Pete tells me you were a schoolteacher back in Indiana. Did you enjoy it?" Alice asked a little later after everyone had stopped to have a bite to eat.

"I enjoyed it very much, and if Ben and I had not decided to become wayfarers, I would probably be there in front of my class right now. Some of my students went to our church, and many were relatives, so they got to see 'Aunt Peggy' every day. I do miss them terribly."

Alice sipped her tea and chuckled. "The reason I ask is that we are going to need a new schoolteacher in Cantana. I have been teaching the school here for the last several years, but I am so busy with the hotel and restaurant and town responsibilities I've taken on that, well, it has become needful for me to give it up." She paused, her expression serious. "Would this be something you might be interested in?"

Peggy's face seemed to brighten as she looked over at Ben. "I . . . I might be interested, but Ben and I need to discuss it first. Would that be all right?"

"That would be fine, Peg. Right now we are holding classes at Granfield House, but we want to convert one of the empty buildings in town to a schoolhouse and also use it to hold church services on Sundays. If you accept the position, you will take over just after the first of the year." Alice smiled. "Let me know what you decide, and I'll discuss the particulars with you. It certainly would be nice to have a new schoolteacher in Cantana."

* * *

Alice stood out on the steps of Granfield House and watched the approaching stage in the distance making its way to town in a fury. Its infrequent trips to Cantana were mostly to drop off the mail and deliver a few packages to the merchants in town. She never knew how many passengers would be aboard, if any, but she needed to be ready to serve them just in case, or at least have food ready for the driver and his shotgun guard.

Stopping in front of Granfield House, the driver opened the stage door and announced that hot victuals could be obtained at the hotel, which was a mere "stretch of the limbs" down the boardwalk. Hearing the driver say "limbs," the word used in polite society in place of "legs" when ladies were present, Alice grinned. It would seem there was at least one woman aboard.

Sure enough, a young lady not yet twenty years old, with blonde hair and a stylish hat, stepped out of the stage door and looked about her. She was fashionably attired with her hair done up in the latest updo reminiscent of the so-called Gibson Girl. Alice greeted her and asked her to

41

take a seat inside and she would see to her trunk and room.

Since there was not a postmaster in Cantana, Alice had added the caring and distribution of the mail to the long list of her other duties in the town. Pete stepped out of his office to help her carry the luggage and several packages inside, not really noticing the passenger who was seated near the lobby door.

Until she called out his name.

"Pete?" Pete turned and was surprised to see Judith Farnsworth, the daughter of the missionaries to the Nez Perce in the Bear Paw Mountains. He hardly recognized her. She had matured into a lovely young woman, a far cry from the thin and wasted teenage girl dressed in tattered rags he had known several years ago in the Bear Paws.

Setting down his burden, Pete held her by the shoulders as she stood up and untied the ribbon from under her chin that secured her hat.

"Hello, young lady! I wondered if I would ever see you again. What made you decide to come back?" he asked, genuinely pleased to see her. She had been as much a part of the adventure to the Bear Paws as Tom and Arliss.

Judith blushed and smiled. "Well, I did come for a visit, but . . . please tell me, Pete—is Tom Brumett still around?"

Pete kept his face from falling with a little effort. "Judith, let's get you settled in first. You must be tired after a long train ride and that confounded stage. You can have a bath and supper, and then we can talk about old times." He tried to smile, wondering how he was going to tell her that Tom Brumett had been sent to Cuba and maybe thereafter to the Philippines to doctor those soldiers fighting in the war—and more to the point, that he was married.

7
PEEDY

Late one evening while doing his rounds, Deputy Hamilton heard a clanking noise and saw the flickering of a kerosene lantern behind Hester's big barn. Stealthily making his way to investigate, he found Arliss Moore working on a wagon in the dark. Having not met him yet, Ben introduced himself.

"Ben Hamilton from Indiana," he said, reaching out to shake hands. "You must be Mr. Moore. Pete has told me a lot about you."

Arliss wiped his greasy fingers on his pant leg and stretched out his hand. "You're the new deputy. Glad to meet you. I work for Bill Hester. Right now, I'm trying to convert this old wagon into a blacksmith's rig so I can service the horses and mules at the surrounding ranches and farms."

Ben walked around the wagon as Arliss held his lantern up high. "I never saw anything like that back home. Is this your idea?"

"Sort of, but we had something like it in the cavalry.

44

Really comes in convenient when a horse throws a shoe away from the fort," Arliss said.

"That will be quite the handy craft, Mr. Moore. I'd like to see it when you've completed it," Ben said with a grin.

"I'd be obliged if you would call me Arliss. When folks address me by my last name, I think I'm back in the army again," he said. "This little rig should save the ranchers time and bother knowing that by appointment, a blacksmith will come out to them and care for their stock on such and such a day. It adds value to my work that they don't mind paying for."

"Well, Godspeed, Arliss, I'll let you get back to your task," Ben said, pinching the brim of his hat. "I'll have to have you over for supper some night." And as the young deputy walked back to the main street of town, Arliss sat down on the edge of the wagon wheel that he had removed to grease the bearing, thoughtful about life in Cantana and how he planned to fit into it.

* * *

Late one evening when Arliss was eating supper with Bill Hester, he decided to discuss some of his plans for the future. "Bill, I've noticed that old freight wagon you have setting out back. Is that spoken for?"

Bill smiled. "That old war wagon has been out back for years. It used to belong to the lumber yard before they went bust. They owed me money and this was all I could get out of them. Did you take a good look at it? It's huge! Gotta be 'most twelve feet long with open sides, able to haul six or seven thousand pounds of lumber or freight. Why do you ask?"

Arliss finished chewing his mouthful of steak. "Bill, you've been mighty kind to me and I want to do right by you so I'll tell you what I have in mind. If you will let me work off the price of that wagon, I'd like to fix it up and start my own freight business."

Bill Hester picked up a toothpick from the shot glass on the table in front of him, stuck it in his teeth, and pushed himself back in his chair. Staring at Arliss for a few moments, he squinted his eyes and bobbed his head. "Son, I have a proposal for you. I'm not a young man anymore. That day when those two McGuffy brothers came into town, I was about all done in. If you hadn't helped me, well . . . I'm lookin' to retire, sell the business and move to Fargo to live out the rest of my days with my daughter and grandkids. I was thinkin' of sellin' the business to you. You're young and one of the best dern farriers I've ever seen. It would go along perfect with your freight business. Tell you what—I'll give ya the freight wagon now for free as a sign of good faith. What do ya say?"

Arliss put down his fork. "Did I just hear right? You'd be willing to sell me your business? But I couldn't afford it! I don't have that kind of money!"

Bill Hester smiled. "Arliss, I've been able to put by a few dollars over the years so I'm not desperate for cash. We can work out payments that you can send me every month. I know all about you, son. You are an honorable man," Bill said. "Marshal Randers says so."

"But I have no collateral, no money to put down," Arliss said, his brain feeling as light as a feather.

"Down payment is one dollar! And what you did for me that day with the McGuffy boys is your collateral," Bill said. "Go ahead and sleep on it. We can draw up papers and have Pete witness them if ya want. Now, let's have some of that apple pie I brought from Granfield House."

* * *

Arliss worked on the old freight wagon when he could, sometimes far into the night. He also leased the long-abandoned freight office several doors down Main Street that was owned by the town. It was Arliss's idea to take over the freight deliveries between Cantana and Havre and maybe establish a few routes between some of the depots along the Hi-line to the smaller outlying towns. He knew the larger, established freight companies didn't want to bother taking supplies to Cantana, which was nothing but a deadhead run to the Canadian border with nothing to show for the return trip but an empty wagon. This added significantly to the price of freight which had to be passed on to the customers, further adding to the cost of living on the remote prairie. If Arliss could successfully haul freight and later warehouse supplies out of Cantana, the costs would be lower, and the town's essentials would always be available, even through a bitter Montana winter.

But where to start? Arliss knew about horses and mules and blacksmithing; he knew about wagons and freight but how was he to let the merchants in town know what he proposed to do? Scratching his head with the pencil he had been making notes with since early that morning, he suddenly had an idea. Walking down the street he came to the fancy French doors of Granfield House.

"Alice?" Arliss said, standing at the hotel's guest counter. "Do you have time for a talk?"

Alice came out from her office. "Why of course. How may I help you?" she asked.

"Pete must have told you of my idea of starting a freight business. I would like to make up some handbills to pass out to merchants to advertise and wondered if you could help me. I have some ideas but am not sure where to begin. You're good at this sort of thing," Arliss said. "This is all new to me and maybe it's just a pipe dream. Maybe those folks won't want to do business with me."

Alice smiled. "Nonsense! You have something good to offer and they have a need for it. Let's have a seat in the dining room.

Finding the small round table in the back corner that

Alice always used to do her paperwork, she asked the server to bring them coffee and some sweet rolls.

"The first thing we must do is establish goodwill with these merchants in Cantana so they will trust you. Granfield House will be your first customer. That should give you some pull. Secondly, you must make it profitable for them to use your services. You'll want them to think of you as a square dealer. And if you can garner a good reputation, word will soon get around and this might persuade new residents to locate here and start new businesses," Alice said, reading the notes that Arliss had made and then making a few of her own. Soon, Alice had an attractive handbill sketched out that the printer in town could follow.

Arliss's head was swimming. He could for the first time see the possibilities of his dream coming to fruition and it made him feel real good. And Alice was feeding that dream by her assistance. Arliss had never been able to work for another man very long because he needed his freedom. And the only way he could maintain the freedom to which he had grown accustomed was by working for the only boss who had never let him down—Arliss Moore.

Several weeks later and after working more than a few nights through to dawn, the repairs to the old wagon were completed. Bill Hester inspected the work and proclaimed that he couldn't have done better himself. He suggested to Arliss that he start hauling freight right away.

"Winter will be comin' soon, and the quicker you can haul a couple of loads the better," he said. Arliss liked the idea and agreed. The income would allow him to settle up with Bill just that much sooner and to fix up living quarters for himself in the old freight office.

Freshly painting the box and frame of the large wagon in dark blue with a new white canvas, he painted the wheels yellow to emulate the colors of the cavalry. Neatly printed on both sides in white lettering were the words: **ARLISS MOORE FREIGHTERS.**

Arliss was dubious at first about making his company a plural, since he had only the one wagon, but this was his ambition, and he would leave the company name as he had painted it. Parking the wagon out in front of the livery stable where all could get a good look, he let the town know that he was ready for business.

The merchants in Cantana openly voiced their support for him but secretly wondered if he could do it. Arliss's hopes were high, and though he had not yet delivered one package, he planned to soon purchase a second freight wagon with his profits and put another man on it. He might even be able to supply some of the towns across the Canadian border if he could establish his reputation . . . but he was getting ahead of himself.

* * *

Having no commitments for several days, he decided that it was now or never, and with orders in hand from Granfield House, Hester's livery, the Red Angus, Swift's general store, and other assorted small businesses hanging on to their existence by a thread, Arliss struck out for Havre on his maiden voyage.

The weather was soft, and with hard, dry ground his path, Arliss started out with his empty wagon before daybreak, believing he could make it to the tracks by tomorrow noon and then Havre by later that evening. The return trip with a full wagonload would naturally be slower, but he figured to be back in Cantana by the end of the week. He would load the wagon as full as he could without overtaxing the mules. Any empty places in the wagon would be stuffed with chunks of coal so there would be no wasted unprofitable space.

Pete Randers and Tom Brumett had related to him in detail, the circumstances of that fierce winter journey they had made several years before along this same path. How different this ride would be compared to that grueling winter journey to the Bear Paw Mountains.

* * *

Arliss arrived in Havre late the next day as the sun was setting. He pulled in behind the large livery stables to feed and bed his mules for the night. They weren't spring

51

chickens anymore, and he'd worried about them. But after his inspection, they seemed to be no worse for wear from the journey. Perhaps he could, by and by, purchase some more from the army. He would certainly keep his eyes and ears open in his travels for any good deals on mule flesh.

It was very late, but he would try getting himself something to eat and then bed down in his wagon for an early start in the morning. As Arliss walked the boardwalk in the approaching twilight, he knew he had to be careful. Although he was a formidable, intimidating figure himself, he was no match for a crowd of liquored-up cowboys itching to have their way with a lone black man.

Arliss wanted to locate the supply warehouses near the edge of town to save him time in the morning and find a place that would serve him his supper. If that was not possible, he would have some cold beef and sourdough bread he'd brought along and reheat his cold coffee from earlier in the day. Assuring himself of the warehouse's location, Arliss cut through a narrow alleyway cluttered up with old wooden crates and scrap lumber used for kindling to keep the fires burning in the saloons.

As he stepped quickly to find his way to his wagon, something burst out of the darkness, striking him across the legs. Arliss pulled his revolver and cocked the hammer, his heart pounding in his chest. Bright light from an open doorway flashed, revealing that it had only been a feral cat startled at his approach. Smiling to himself that he would pull a gun on a cat, he reholstered his revolver only to notice further movement among the wooden crates. Thinking it might be a cowboy sleeping off his drink, Arliss cautiously approached the place . . . only to be surprised to hear the muffled sound of someone weeping.

"Come out of there where I can see you," he spoke, his hand gripping the handle of his .45 Colt. There was more movement as the source of the tears stood up. To Arliss's surprise, it was a young black boy of about ten or eleven holding a kitten in his arms. His tears glistened on his cheeks in the poor light of the alleyway. Arliss stooped down in front of the child.

"Boy, what you doin' here hidin' in the dark? Why you cryin'?"

The child sniffed hard, wiping his nose on his sleeve. "I'm scared. It's dark, an' I'm cold."

"Where's your momma?" Arliss asked as the child peered into his face, just as surprised to see the tall, black cowboy standing before him as the cowboy was to see him.

"Ain't got no momma—no daddy neither," the boy said, sniffing his runny nose and brushing away the tears from his eyes.

Arliss reached out, lifting the boy's cap. "Then where do you live? Ain't you got no home?"

"No, sir. I come here from Chicago lookin' to find some new folks. My momma and daddy are dead, so I hid out on the train to come west. I heared that orphlins could find new folks out in the West."

"When did you eat last, son?"

"This mornin' sir; I knocked on a back door up the alleyway and a nice white lady giv'd me some biscuits and gravy."

Arliss stood up and pressed his lips together, looking up into the vastness of the Montana night sky as if trying to locate heaven for advice. "All right, then, come along with me—bring your cat. What's your name, son?"

"It's Peedy, sir. Are you goin' to take me to the police?"

"No . . . no. I don't know what I'm going to do with you, but let me leastwise get you some victuals. I've got something in the wagon, not as good as those biscuits and gravy you had this morning, but it will fill your little belly."

Arliss watched as the foundling gobbled down a thick slice of cold beef pressed between some plain bread and butter and washed it down with cool water. Apparently the little boy had heard of the orphan trains that traveled out west and thought he could find himself a new set of parents, not yet understanding that a black child had little chance of finding an arrangement like that out here. If he did manage to find someone to take him in, he would most likely not be anyone's real son but would end up a servant—sweeping floors, running errands, emptying chamber pots, and polishing spittoons.

Watching the boy eat and then curl up with his cat in the corner of the wagon all tuckered out, Arliss covered him up with his old wool army blanket. He knew the chances of finding any black folks in north-central Montana to take this boy in were next to nothing. Arliss had no choice but to take him along. He had freight to haul and customers to win over, but at least Peedy would be safe with him until he could figure out what to do with him.

* * *

Early the next morning, Arliss and Peedy hitched up the mules from the livery. Paying the blacksmith, he took Peedy by the hand and walked him down the long boardwalk to a small eating house that he knew might serve them a meal. Arliss took a seat in the corner where he could have his back to the wall and lifted Peedy into a chair next to him. He had purchased a small basket with a lid earlier that morning for Peedy to keep his cat in so he could leave it back at the wagon.

There were not many people in the establishment at that time of morning, and as they waited, a handsome middle-aged woman approached their table, matronly in form and dress with long brown wispy hair pinned back and up.

"Well, Sergeant Moore, I haven't seen you for quite some time. Not in the army anymore, I see. Is this your son?" the woman inquired with a gentle smile.

"No, Mrs. Hays. I'm on my own now, and this young

fellow here is Peedy, a friend of mine. I remembered how kind you were to us men of the 10th and thought we might get breakfast this morning."

"But I've met Peedy before, haven't I?" Mrs. Hays said, touching the boy's face with the coolness of her hand. "I didn't know his name then, but I know he likes biscuits and gravy. What can I get you fine gentlemen this morning?"

Arliss smiled. "We'll both have some more of those biscuits and gravy, some fried eggs, and some bread. I'll have coffee, and Peedy here will have a tall glass of milk. Will that suit you, son?" Arliss nudged the small boy in the ribs. He returned a giggle.

"Coming right up, gentlemen," Mrs. Hays said as she made her way back to the kitchen.

"Mr. Arliss? That was the nice lady who giv'd me breakfast yesterday," Peedy said, tugging the large man's sleeve.

"I figured it was Mrs. Hays when you told me," Arliss responded. "When I was in the army, Mrs. Hays would serve us colored troops of the 10th Cavalry our meals when we came to town. She is a fine lady and has a large heart. Her husband was an old cavalry soldier killed in battle many years ago."

Soon the food arrived, and Arliss and his young companion wasted no time. It was hot and good and reminded Arliss that there were still plenty of kind people in the world. He settled his bill at the counter before leaving and as Mrs. Hays gave him his change, she handed a large brown paper sack to Peedy.

"It's a long drive back to the border, I know. Here are some sandwiches to tide you over—compliments of the house, shall we say."

Arliss pinched the brim of his hat and smiled. "Obliged, ma'am. Your kindness won't be soon forgotten."

As Arliss turned to leave, his eyes caught glimpse of a tall young woman standing by the door to the back kitchen, her arms folded loosely across her waist as she stared back at him in silence. She was pretty, he thought; her hair shiny and black in tight curls and her skin the color of fine maple syrup, beaded with perspiration from the heat of the stove. Arliss surmised she was the cook, and he tried to send her a smile, but she did not smile back. Only her eyes followed after him as he took Peedy by the shoulder and walked him out the door.

Arliss did not remember seeing her or any other women of color while stationed at Fort Assiniboine or in the course of his many visits to town. *Likely she is already spoken for,* he thought.

* * *

The large wagon finally loaded, Arliss thumbed through his list of orders to be sure he had not missed anything. Satisfied, he and Peedy stopped at the post office to check

57

on the mail for Cantana. Handing the postmaster a letter signed by Marshal Randers that gave him proxy to retrieve the mail for the town, he inserted a bundle of letters and several packages in a canvas bag. Peedy asked if he could carry the bag. Smiling, Arliss looped the strap over the small boy's shoulders. "Not too heavy?" he asked.

"No, sir—not too heavy," the young boy answered.

Arliss lifted Peedy up onto the seat next to him and noticed that he was wheezing and sniffing and that his sleeve was shiny and slick from wiping his nose. He held Peedy's chin in his massive hand, tilting his head back to examine him. "It looks like you got the hay fever, boy. I'll fix you up with some nostrum as soon as we can make camp."

It was early afternoon when Arliss stopped his freight wagon in a low spot only several miles north of town. Lifting Peedy to the ground, he grabbed his shovel from the bracket on the side of the wagon and began digging a fire pit. Placing several chunks of coal in the hole on a bed of sticks and dry grass he had gathered as kindling, he splashed some kerosene from the lantern that hung from the wagon and lit the fire. As the wood burned, the coal soon ignited, producing a steady, almost smokeless heat.

Putting a pot of water on to boil, Arliss motioned for Peedy to follow him as he walked a few hundred yards along the shallow depression near the camp. On a small grassy hill were several dozen tall plants, some almost as tall as Arliss. Breaking off one of the plants at its base, Arliss began to remove its large green fleshy leaves along the bottom and the yellow flowers and buds from the spike-like top.

"Here's something for you to learn, boy. These plants grow might nigh everywhere—all over the country I've heard. They are called mullein and are easy to find. The Indians and the cowboys use the yellow flowers to make a tea—cures a lot of things, including the hay fever. The leaves come in handy too, to clean your bottom after you do your business, if you know what I mean. Remember that when you are out by yourself with no one to help you."

As they walked back to camp, Arliss continued, "And you surely don't have to wipe your nose on your sleeve." Reaching under the seat of his wagon, he opened a wooden toolbox he kept there and brought out a small package wrapped in brown paper and tied up with white string. "Here, son, this is for you to have."

Peedy looked at Arliss in surprise. Setting down his kitten, he untied the string and slowly unwrapped the brown paper, removing the contents. It was a yellow handkerchief that was almost large enough for Peedy to hide behind. The image of a brown buffalo was embroidered at one corner with the number 10 above it, evidently from Arliss's days as a buffalo soldier with the 10th U.S. Cavalry.

"Nobody ever giv'd me nothin' before," Peedy said. "It's

too nice to wipe my nose on."

Arliss smiled. "You go ahead and don't worry about that. We can wash it when it gets soiled. I've had that thing for a long time, and I'm glad to see someone finally getting the use of it."

8

CHRISTMAS AT GRANFIELD HOUSE

It was Christmas Eve on the prairie, and how beautiful. Pete bundled his heavy scarf about his neck and face and made his way down the boardwalk through the foot or so of snow that had been falling for the last several days. His steps were muffled as he made his round of the town before heading to celebrate Christmas with Alice, her parents, and close friends.

Pete was most concerned about the Red Angus saloon and those who might seek refuge there from the weather, desiring to make merry with too much drink. But when he walked through the front door and gazed about him, he could see that most of the weary cowboys had already gone upstairs to sleep. A few hands were still seated close to the stove, playing cards and keeping warm. Others were eating their roast beef and gravy, a special treat prepared by Jack Macgregor in keeping with the holiday. All seemed well, and the town was quiet.

As Pete stomped his feet and entered the French doors of the dining room of Granfield House, he thought about his good friend Captain Tom Brumett, sent off to ply his skills as a medical doctor in the war against Spain. Disappointed was the girl left behind, Judith Farnsworth, now a temporary resident or perhaps a prisoner of Cantana. She was living alone at Granfield House. After arriving several months ago on the train from Chicago, Judith had discovered to her dismay that Brumett had married another before departing, leaving her shaken and unsure of her future path.

Among the guests that evening were Arliss Moore and Peedy, the Hamiltons, the Swifts, Bill Hester, and Dan LaForge of the North-West Mounted Police, serendipitously close enough to Montana that day to enjoy a few hours of Christmas cheer at Granfield House. Dan would be departing in the deep snow and cold in only a few hours so he vied to make the best of it. It wouldn't be too hard, especially given he had taken great interest in the person of Judith Farnsworth.

The grand, festive supper was too soon over as the guests repaired to the large sitting room to hear Alice's father, Richard Granfield, do his annual reading of *A Christmas Carol* by the late British author Charles Dickens. This was fast becoming an annual tradition at Granfield House. The lamps were turned down low and only the candles allowed to burn brightly to illuminate the pies and cakes on the long buffet table awaiting the guests' attention upon completion of the book.

Children were seated around the room along the floor to hear the Christmas ghost story. They squirmed impatiently as their thoughts were continually drawn away to the white boiled frosting and butter cream fillings of the cakes adorned with sugary fruits. The children tried to contain themselves, earnestly listening to the book's five chapters, or *staves* as Dickens called them, having been taught to listen for those final words: "And so, as Tiny Tim observed, God Bless Us, Every One!"

Dan LaForge listened to the familiar words of the popular novella, remembering the stories his father had told him of Francis Dickens, the son of the great author who had been a member of the North-West Mounted Police. Dan's father had known him while stationed at Fort Walsh.

Francis Dickens's life had not been a happy one, and after retirement from the force, he was to have begun a new career on the lecture circuit, an endeavor that had proven highly successful for his father. Sadly, he died of a heart attack at a friend's home in Moline, Illinois, and was buried there before his own career really began. Dan thought how strange it was as a Canadian to be linked to Charles Dickens, the great Victorian author of England, by this simple and fragile thread of life.

Soon the reading was over, and with the lights turned up again, plates of cake and pie and cups of coffee, tea, and cocoa were made ready for the mingling guests. Dan spotted Judith Farnsworth seated across the room and made his way to her side.

"What are your plans then, Miss Farnsworth?" he inquired after seating himself next to her on the davenport. "Will you soon be returning to Chicago or remain here?"

Judith smiled. "I don't know yet, sir," she answered. "Perhaps I will return there in the spring. My plans for now are just to remain inside and keep warm." She smiled at her own blandly humorous remark. "Perhaps I can help around the hotel. I am accustomed to hard work, and sitting around idle for long periods of time does not suit me. What about you, Corporal LaForge? What does the future hold for a mounted policeman?"

Mildly surprised when the searchlight was turned on him, LaForge leaned back in his place, thoughtfully balancing his cup and saucer on his knee. "I'm not sure, Miss Farnsworth. Word has it that I may soon be promoted to sergeant and offered a small detachment of my own. Then perhaps I may get married and have children . . . if someone will have me," he said with a smile. "Or I might go to the Yukon and help police the gold rush, or be prevailed upon to sail to Africa and fight the Boers."

Nothing Dan had said seemed to get a rise from Judith, who sat quietly looking at him as if he were a painting or a sculpture instead of flesh and blood. He could have very well added to his list of ambitions that he expected to be named prime minister of Canada, and it would have made no apparent difference to her. All at once he felt like a schoolboy trying to impress his freckle-faced girlfriend by hanging upside down from a tree branch. He said nothing more.

Finally, as if her mind had been occupied elsewhere, Judith spoke. "Well, sir. That is quite ambitious, is it not?"

Dan and Judith chatted for awhile about life in Canada, and as their conversation eventually drifted and waned due to the lateness of the hour, she stood and excused herself for the night, thanking LaForge for his company. "Sir, I don't know when I shall see you again, but we have certainly had a nice talk. I wish I could have been better company. My mind has been preoccupied of late."

"I only come through occasionally," Dan explained, standing up. "Like bad weather. If I get that promotion and assignment, I may not be able to come this way for a long time, if ever."

Judith chewed her bottom lip in thought. "Well, sir. I'm sure you will have departed long before the morning light. I will pray for you, and I hope your promotion does not come too soon, so that haply I will get to see and speak with you again." She reached out to offer her hand. "I hope I will be here when you come back through. You seem to be a gentleman."

Encouraged, Dan said, "I feel the same way. I would like to see you again also. And I hope you fight off any urge to return to Chicago before I can come back."

He cleared his throat. "At the risk of sounding brazen, I've wanted to tell you that I heard about your life in the Bear Paw Mountains from Pete and from my father . . . of your dedication to those Indians and your bravery when your parents were killed. I have admired you in spirit, even though I'd never met you before now."

Then with a stammering, he paused. "Detachment life is not for everyone, and it can be especially hard on the women. Besides normal domestic duties, the wives of the men are often called upon to double as cooks for the prisoners and the other policemen assigned there, serving as nurses and oft-times jailers, caring for the needs of sordid men locked up in crude jail cells made of rough-cut boards built in their very own living rooms. The wife of a mounted policeman is also his deputy at these secluded detachments. But I was thinking . . . what an amazing wife you would make for some lonely man, banished to the backside of the wilderness—or for some lonely mounted policeman!"

Judith sucked in her breath and held it, blinking, and with a quick nod of her head, bid him good night as she swiftly vacated the room. Dan watched her vanish up the stairs, knowing immediately in his heart that he had misread her and overstepped his privilege. He hoped no one else had seen the private exchange as he wished everyone in the room a Merry Christmas before retiring, anticipating the few short hours of miserable, restless sleep before him and an early departure into the cold and snow.

9
PETE STRETCHES HIMSELF

Pete had been able to wrangle cooperation from the merchants and suppliers along the Hi-line when he was first promoted to marshal of the town. Encouraged by these earlier successes, he thought he could twist a few more arms and get the long sought after and promised railroad spur put in and the telegraph line repaired. If he could manage that, Cantana might be a real town again and maybe someday a great city.

Paying a visit to Alice who was busy in her office at Granfield House, Pete decided to enlist her help writing a carefully worded letter to the head of the railroad. "I wonder about Mr. Hill. What kind of person do you really think he is? I know he's a great business man and all, but certainly he didn't become a great man by making promises that he did not intend to keep. That sort of thing catches up with you after a while," Pete said thoughtfully.

"Likely he has a lot on his plate. Maybe he just needs reminding. We are all like that sometimes. When he reads this letter it might bring it all back," Alice answered.

Pete shifted in his chair. "From my point of view, he doesn't seem like the kind of person who would build a spur and repair a telegraph line for nothing. I've heard that Mr. Hill does not like to lay unnecessary track and that he actually scouted out the path for the Hi-line railroad himself to find the shortest route, not giving a hoot or holler about providing beautiful scenery for his passengers".

A server came in with a tray of coffee and cookies. Pete poured a cup for himself and Alice, taking a quick sip.

"Maybe in this letter, I can get him to agree to meet with us in Havre. It is said he comes through Montana regularly. If we can get him to fix the telegraph, then maybe we can nail him down to putting in the spur. Sometimes people find it hard to say no when you are looking at them face-to-face," Alice said cheerfully. "I can be hopeful."

But a terse reply came several weeks later by stage, apparently answered by a subordinate of Mr. Hill's. The meeting was flatly refused and the telegraph repairs not even mentioned. The letter was caustic at best, ending with the postscript: "Let the cattlemen bring their stock to the railroad like everyone else!"

Pete was angry at the arrogant dismissal, and he vowed to begin a letter-writing campaign from one end of Montana to the other. The next stage through Cantana was

69

given a canvas bag full of letters addressed to every newspaper across northern Montana, including some of the larger papers in the East. Alice said nothing, quietly helping Pete write, but was dubious that a David from the town of Cantana could force the Goliath of the railroad to do his bidding. Giants were very capable of crushing things smaller than themselves. Perhaps Pete was asking for trouble.

Pete did not really know what he expected to happen when he began his crusade, but as the days and weeks went by with no response, it appeared that the newspapers had ignored him too. Not understanding subtle politics and just how intimidating someone of Mr. Hill's eminence could be, even to a large newspaper, Pete was beginning to realize that Cantana's problems were but a tempest in the proverbial teapot compared to a country at war.

* * *

One cold spring morning, Pete and Ben rode out east of town to settle a dispute between a rancher and a farmer. The farmer complained that the rancher's cattle had gotten into his garden. The rancher claimed it was open range and he was not responsible for what his cattle might do.

"Sam," Pete said to the rancher. "Can't you find a way to settle this with Higgins? I know that ranchers are not supposed to like sodbusters but he is your neighbor, and if I remember right, Mrs. Higgins was there for you when your wife gave birth to your little girl. Now why don't you take a day, bring over your boys and build them a fence around their garden and help them replant it. It's no skin off your nose and the folks around here will think mighty fine of you for it."

Sam Saunders removed his hat and smoothed his hair back in thought. Then a smile shone across his face. "I'd forgotten about Mrs. Higgins," he said with a grin. "I'll do it. I'll go talk to Higgins myself. Maybe we can make a barbecue out of it."

Pete and Ben shook hands with the rancher and rode back west to Cantana. "That was a fair piece of diplomacy, Pete. You sometimes remind me of my old chief back in Indiana. He was always getting people at odds to drink from the same trough," Ben said.

Pete smiled but thought to himself. *Yeah, but I can't get the railroad to keep its promises.*

Clearing his throat, Pete pulled Sadie closer to his deputy's horse. "Ben, I know I've been spending a lot of time on this railroad thing. I'm sorry for that. It's been a dream of mine for a long time to see this town prosper but it's got me licked, and I've let myself sink up to my hips in politics instead of concentrating on my job as a lawman. I'm ready to settle down and do the job I was hired to do," Pete said.

71

Ben smiled and nodded as they stopped off to have dinner at Granfield House.

10
DAN'S PREROGATIVE

It had been almost three months since Dan celebrated Christmas Eve at Granfield House, and though constrained by duty to leave the following morning before first light, he had enjoyed those precious few hours with his American friends. He lived and relived them in his times alone, which were many. What an occasion it had been to make merry with a good meal, a warm bed and bath, and a chance to sing Christmas carols around the piano as he had done living in Regina with his father and mother as a young boy. Now his folks were in Oregon, too far away for him to visit or see them often. He had no other close family, and except for chums he had grown up with and fellow members of the force, his closest friends were these Americans living close enough to Canada to spit over the border.

Pete Randers had attempted to explain Judith's situation to Dan, perhaps unintentionally *telling tales out of school* of her unexpected return to Montana with the notion of renewing her friendship with Tom Brumett. Had it been in her mind to surprise Tom, thinking he would always be willing and waiting for her? Whatever had been her intentions, she had failed to keep up with his letters, leading him to believe that any chance for them was over. Now Tom Brumett had moved on forever.

Dan had not acquired much experience with courting, growing up in an almost cloistered paramilitary environment around the Old Depot in Regina. This was obvious by his failure to appreciate Judith's feelings over Tom Brumett, and when he'd seen what he thought was an opportunity, he'd practically suggested to her face that she could drop everything, follow him back to Canada, and take up housekeeping with him as his wife.

Three months later, he was still raking himself over the coals for it. With such clumsy tactics, Dan shouldn't have been surprised when Judith fled from his presence like a frightened dove.

* * *

It was a clear, cold March morning along the Frenchman River, southwest of the small town of Eastend, located less than forty miles north of the United States border in the territorial land soon to become the province of Saskatchewan. Eastend was the starting point of a clandestine assignment given to Corporal LaForge by his inspector.

Headquarters had been receiving information that

young girls were being held against their will at some of the wilderness trading posts. The reports were nonspecific except that they involved establishments south of Eastend to the Montana border. It was Dan's job to investigate and take action if warranted. Provisioned and with his special orders tucked securely inside a hidden pocket of his coat, he set out westward along the river to fulfill his mission.

In place of his usual police uniform of red serge, Dan wore the soiled, shabby clothing of a trapper and hunter, topped with a scruffy beard and fur cap. His horse and saddle were borrowed and bore no markings of the North-West Mounted Police. His official uniform and accoutrements were carefully folded and secreted in the baggage tied to the back of the pack mule that trailed patiently behind him. It had been the idea of his inspector for him to proceed incognito and to begin his trail from some remote location to allay suspicion.

Working his way along the south shore of the Frenchman River, Dan sought to hasten his ride and avoid discovery by staying clear of the shoreline and its loops and meanders until well away from town. If he was being watched or followed, it might compromise his mission and put him in a situation where he would have to defend himself alone against an unknown number of miscreants.

Dan remembered well the story his father had told him of the American army sergeant who helped him out of a tough spot when his partner was killed by whiskey traders from the States. It was the beginning of a lifelong friendship between an American cavalry sergeant who became a prairie marshal and a sergeant of the Mounties. But he could not hope for anything like that out here on his own, many miles north of Montana in the sparsely populated wilderness. Nevertheless, his mission was meant to be covert, and he was expected to do his duty—unaided and alone.

The sun began its trek above the horizon. As the long shadows retreated, Dan watched intently behind him. He was a stranger to these parts and might be viewed with great distrust by other hunters and trappers. Pausing occasionally in the shadows of trees along the river, he saw nothing but a few partridges and a noisy woodpecker, tapping away his serenade on wood in honor of the new day. A small herd of deer grazing along the water were unalarmed and unconcerned by what was about them. Dan believed he was alone and had been able to depart the small town unnoticed.

Starting out again, he followed the Frenchman River as it turned sharply southward. Dan's plan was to begin with the first place he came to below Eastend, checking thereafter at each subsequent location on his list, crisscrossing the Canadian wilds as he worked his way southward.

As the day was almost spent and the sun hung low in the western sky, Dan began to look for a suitable spot to set up his camp. Except for patches of snow, the ground was mostly dry. Coming upon a stream of clean, rushing water, he fed and watered his horse and mule. Tying them up in a sheltered place out of the wind where they could nibble upon dried grass at their leisure, Dan quickly dug a small fire pit. Filling his coffeepot with water and hanging it from a hook fastened to a metal tripod over the blaze, he threw in a handful of coffee grounds from his small hand grinder.

Earlier that day, Dan had come across several families of Métis living along the river. Métis were indigenous people of Canada, usually the descendants of marriages between Native women and white settlers. They were famous for their skill at making pemmican, and Dan bought several pounds from them. Traditionally made from dried buffalo meat, melted suet, and sometimes dried berries, pemmican could be very delicious made into a stew called *rubaboo*. Since the buffalo were almost gone, Dan surmised that this particular batch was probably elk meat with some dried wild cranberries mixed in.

Setting his frying pan on the hot coals of the fire, Dan broke off a large piece of the pemmican he stored in a leather bag and stirred it on the hot surface of the pan with a wooden spoon. As the congealed mixture began to melt and break apart, he shook a quantity of dried onion from a glass jar he kept in his bag into the palm of his hand. Slicing in two parsnips, he stirred the stew until everything was tender and then added a cup of water. Not having any flour

77

to act as thickener, he broke up a bannock cake given to him by one of the Métis women. As he stirred, the stew bubbled, steamed, and thickened.

Adding more wood to the fire, he laid out his bedroll next to a tree by the stream. And sitting down on it with his cup of black coffee on his knee, he ate his supper from the frying pan, thankful for hot, tasty food and a place to sleep as the chill of the evening set in.

* * *

Over a period of days and weeks, Dan had been diligent in his investigations and was therefore surprised when he could find nothing out of place. All of the females he encountered were owner's wives and daughters or other family members operating their establishments in a more or less normal and legal manner. Carefully and casually questioning the men at these locations, he heard nothing to make him suspicious. Most of the inns he encountered were little more than log cabins with sleeping space on the floor, simple meals consisting of some sort of pottage of meat, grains, vegetables and bread, and a sparse and basic inventory that might tide one over until he could reach the next trading post.

Dan departed his next-to-last stop en route to his final location not far from the Montana border. It was a small collection of cabins surrounding a fairly large inn where weary trappers could find a place to bed down, get a hot meal, purchase supplies, and barter their furs and skins. There was even a blacksmith out back, banging away and throwing sparks with his hammer. The place had no official name, and its designation wasn't on most of the maps, but it had evidently been built by whiskey traders from Montana. These invaders from the United States, having been cleared out of Canada by the Mounties many years ago, had left these buildings behind to become occupied by some indigenous men of enterprise.

Arriving early in the evening, Dan tied his horse and mule to the rail near the door so he could keep an eye on them. Carefully looking around, he noticed several other horses and mules tied nearby, scratching through the patchy snow to find edible grass. Unfastening the feed bag tied to his mule, Dan filled it with several handfuls of grain and hung it around the mule's head. Next he would feed his horse and then lead them both to water.

Dan walked through the front door of the inn with as little fanfare as possible, carrying his bedroll, rifle, and war bags, hoping that he wouldn't meet anyone he recognized. As his eyes slowly focused in the large, dark room, he looked about him. Spying several rough men seated around a small table playing cards, Dan dropped his things on the floor at his feet. Holding his rifle and leaning against the counter to wait his turn, he watched as the owner discussed the virtues of a new Winchester saddle gun with a customer.

Dan was surprised indeed that this inconspicuous place in the wilds was so well stocked with supplies. Pots and pans hung on the walls along with nearly everything else. Boxes of ammunition filled a long shelf. Fastened to the high wall all along the ceiling were the mounted heads of several black bears and mountain lions, a grizzly bear, and even a white polar bear. Traded furs had been sorted and hung from the walls in the back by leather straps. Barrels of kerosene, lanterns, wool blankets, snowshoes, ready-made clothing, firearms, and a copious selection of spirits filled every nook and narrow space. Bolts of fabric filled several shelves, and a barrel full of hickory axe handles stood in the corner. Shelves and shelves held canned goods: fruits, vegetables, tinned meats, coffee and tea, sacks of flour and sugar, cans of condensed milk, and even a rarer item in the West—Nestlé's Infant Food for babies unable to digest mother's milk.

Dan's first thought was that he hoped he would not discover anything untoward and be forced to interfere with the daily workings of this wilderness trading post, which was obviously very important to the hunters, trappers, woodsman, settlers, Indians, and transients in general around here.

The large man behind the counter seemed friendly enough. He spoke with a heavy Scandinavian accent, possibly Norwegian. Dan quickly thought how handy it would have been to have Pete Randers along—he spoke the language fluently.

"Could I get a bed and some hot grub and drink?" Dan growled.

"No beds; plenty of places on the floor by the fire," the man answered. "Food and drink we have—venison stew and bread—ale to drink, ja?"

"That'll be fine," Dan answered, collecting his property and moving it to the floor by the stove. As he looked about him, he was very aware of being closely scrutinized by the men playing cards. Dan blew his nose loudly and casually wiped the results on the front of his coat with his hand. Seating himself on the floor near the stove with a plop, he shouted. "Let's have that food and drink out here!"

If he was supposed to look like an uncouth backwoodsman, at least he knew how to play the part.

The old proprietor disappeared in the back, and soon to Dan's surprise, a young white girl with blonde hair came out carrying his food. He estimated her age to be in her very early teens, her appearance purposely kept dowdy with a dress made of faded flour sack material. Her yellow hair had been cropped short, perhaps for practical reasons, signifying that her worth had been measured by the menial service she could perform rather than by a parent's love. Her shoes were little more than thin moccasins made of inexpensive dried leather, perhaps from a rabbit or hare.

She handed Dan a heaping plate of hot stew and a

large, frothy tankard of ale. He immediately took several gulps that spilled down his chin into his beard. Letting forth a loud belch, he wiped his mouth and beard with his sleeve. Dan could tell that the girl was fighting the desire to make eye contact with him, but finally, her eyes met his.

He smiled at her. "What's your name?" The girl said nothing but hurried off behind the counter out of sight.

Dan glanced over at the card players, who were no longer looking his way. Setting the ale down next to him on the floor, Dan sniffed the plate of hot stew, wrinkling his nose at the strong gamey smell, and began to eat, slurping the thick gravy from a large wooden spoon. He wiped the plate clean with a heel of hard bread and chewed the thick crust, washing it all down with the upended contents of his tankard.

"Sir, may I take your plate and cup now?" The young girl had returned. She spoke almost perfect English. Dan nodded, wiping his mouth several times with the back of his sleeve while letting forth one more appreciative, convincing belch.

Dan observed the young girl closely. She did not seem in the least bothered by his manners, or rather the lack thereof. He was sure she had seen and heard worse. As the girl turned to leave, Dan reached out and grabbed her wrist. "Tell me, girl. What is your name?"

The young girl froze as her eyes fluttered. "I . . . I am Ellen," she said in a quivering, fearful voice. "Please don't hurt me, sir." Trembling, she twisted herself free from Dan's grip.

"There's no need to be afraid. Is the innkeeper your father? I noticed you have no accent and speak English very well—better than he does."

The girl looked down at the floor, letting her eyes slowly rise to meet Dan's. "My father and I came west from Ontario. He was a country schoolteacher back there and was sick with the consumption. We came west to get the prairie cure and made it this far to the inn before he died. He is buried out back. Olav allows me to live here as a servant to pay my way."

Dan tried to put her at ease with a smile. "How long ago was that?" he asked, careful not to let the others nearby hear his conversation.

"Almost two years, maybe longer than that," she said, slightly agitated. "Sir, I must get about my duties or Olav will be angry. Please—no more questions."

"One more question. Has anyone here, the men that come through here, or Olav, ever hurt you or been unseemly toward you?" He asked it softly, smiling at the little abandoned wisp of a girl.

Ellen looked deeply into Dan's eyes. He could see she understood his meaning.

"Olav is a bit gruff sometimes, but he has been kind to me overall, and he has never struck me or tried to hurt me. Olav watches over me and keeps me safe from the other men. He does not tolerate any shenanigans."

She said it defensively. Dan wanted so badly to reveal himself, to tell the frightened girl that he was a policeman, to allay her fears at his sordid manners and strange, suggestive questions.

Ellen set the soiled dishes down at her feet, and folding her hands in front of her, stared at the floor. She spoke so softly he could hardly hear. "Sir, I don't know who you are, but you don't seem like the others. Your words and manners, though they be rough, are not your own. You are a good man; I can sense it. If you can help me, please get word to the Mounted Police that I am here. I would be so grateful to you."

"Ellen! Work to be done," came Olav's booming, heavily accented voice from the back room. Ellen nodded to Dan and tried to smile before quickly dashing away in obedience to Olav's voice.

Dan went outside to check on his horse and mule before settling in by the fire for the night. As he unwrapped his bedroll and pulled his blanket over him, his thoughts drifted back to the simple mirth he had enjoyed with his friends at Granfield House on Christmas Eve. He wondered about Judith and what she was doing now . . . if she would leave and return to Chicago or stay in Montana to begin her life anew. If he could only see her one more time before she left, maybe to explain his indelicate remarks and make amends.

But the fire was hot and crackling, and he was that weary. "Judith," he whispered before fading off to the sounds of the men snoring in their various octaves.

* * *

Unable to read his pocket watch against the fading glow of the coals in the stove, Dan struck a match. It was almost five o'clock. Dark and bitter cold outside. He gazed across the shadowy room, detecting a faint glow from a lantern in the back where Ellen and Olav were about to begin their day. The other men who slept on the floor in the dark began to stir. Their hoarse coughs and clearing of throats mixed with the unpleasant odors they emitted soon prompted Dan to get up, collect his things, and go outside to check on his horse and mule.

Leading them off in the distance among a stand of trees, Dan unpacked a bag from the mule, and the best he could in the chill and steadily growing morning light, he shaved his beard in some icy water, careful not to nick himself. Standing behind the mule, he unfolded his red serge, pistol belt, pants, and brown boots, wiping them down with a cloth before dressing. Finally, clipping his white lanyard to the butt of his revolver, stabbing it in its holster, and securing the flap, he finished his adornment: he smoothed and corrected the pinch of his Stetson, and putting on his gloves, he led his animals back to the rail in front of the entrance.

The sun was soon to spill over the horizon as Corporal LaForge pushed open the door to the inn, standing with the glowing dawn behind him. As he expected, everyone stopped, stared, and wondered what his presence should mean.

"Olav?" he shouted to the large Norwegian who had been working in the back and was now approaching the counter. "I am here to take the young girl Ellen back with me to return her to her home."

Olav's mouth gaped in surprise. He began to stammer unintelligibly in his mother tongue, then quickly collected himself, shouting and pointing his finger into Dan's face. "You do not have a right! Her father left her to me!"

Dan knocked Olav's hand out of the way, prompting the other men in the room to rise to their feet.

"Sir, I have orders to take into custody anyone I see fit. In short—it's my prerogative. You have a nice place here, and you provide a great service to those around, but mark my words, sir, in the name of the crown, I will certainly have you in irons if you interfere."

The room grew silent as Olav backed away, and the other men in the room gradually lost interest, turning their attention back to breakfast and hot coffee.

"Ellen!" Dan shouted. The young girl came quickly from behind the counter. "Gather all your things and dress warmly," he ordered. "I'm going to see that you get back home."

Dan could tell that Ellen was not only surprised but confused, but as the mist cleared, she recognized him, seeing it in his eyes that he was the rough trapper from last evening. Swiftly running to him, she hugged him tightly around the waist. "Last night, I was entertaining an angel unawares!" she said to him, and then she disappeared in the back to gather her things.

* * *

A chilly wind was blowing across the plains, making the ride unpleasant. Dan had wrapped his wool blanket around Ellen as she rode in the saddle in front of him, secure and warm against the open flaps of his buffalo-skin coat. They had eaten a light breakfast together that morning of fried fatback and some cut-up potatoes. Ellen had grown sleepy and dozed most of the way, seemingly content to be with her angel and on her way home.

Dan stopped his horse and mule to let them drink from a spring-fed pool of water before moving on. Ellen was awake and questioned Dan about how she would be getting home.

"Well, honey, I was thinking about putting you on the train. Have you ever been on a train before?"

"Yes, sir," she answered. "My father and I rode most of the way west on the train. That is when my father became sick, and we got off to find help. We could find no doctors, so we purchased an adequate old horse and found ourselves at Olav's inn."

"I see," he said. "Have you ever been to the United States?"

Ellen's eyes grew large. "Oh, no sir! America is too big and wild, and too far away," she said, holding on to Dan's heavy coat more snugly than ever.

"Well, what would you say if I told you we are entering the United States right now?" he asked.

Ellen tried to speak but stammered. "How . . . how can that be?" she answered, carefully peeking over the edge of the horse, expecting to see a heavy black border fixed upon the ground, running in both directions east and west until it faded out of sight. She saw nothing but the ground. She sniffed. The air smelled the same, and the weather had not changed. Perhaps Corporal Dan was teasing her again. This couldn't be America. It looked just like Canada, her home.

Dan pointed ahead. "See all those buildings off in the distance? That is the town of Cantana in the state of Montana. We are headed there right now." Ellen was nervous. "Sir, I am frightened of Americans. I have heard they are an angry, warlike people, doing what they want and taking what they want. Will they not arrest us and put us in jail?"

Dan threw his head back and laughed at the sincere, mature-sounding words coming from such a young girl.

"No, my dear, these people are my friends, and I want you to meet them. How would you like to stay in a nice hotel and sleep in a clean, warm bed tonight?"

As they approached the town, the clouds began to sprinkle. "We'll be under cover in a few minutes, Ellen. Just hold on," Dan said.

Marshal Pete was standing on the boardwalk under shelter of the roof's overhang as Dan and Ellen rode up. "Hey, star packer! Just the man I need to see," Dan shouted, gesturing toward his young rider. "My passenger and I need caring for until I can make arrangements to get her headed back east."

Ellen said nothing but tried to smile. She was nervous and unsure of herself, but taking the cue from Dan, she understood that this man wearing a shiny badge was a friend. Pete reached up and lifted Ellen off the horse. He set her down under the eaves of the marshal's office out of the rain.

"You're always welcome, Danny, and so is your friend. Alice will be glad to see you too. Alice tells me its roast beef and gravy smothered in onions and prairie mushrooms and creamed green beans on the supper menu. Let's get your horse and mule put up at Hester's, and then come with me to supper. Then you can explain your little partner here."

* * *

89

Living almost two years with Olav the Norwegian at his inn, dealing with the sorrow of her father's death and the despair of watching her life go on, day after day, without hope, Ellen felt numb as Corporal Dan took her by the hand to guide her across the street to Granfield House. It had begun to rain harder now as they reached the steps, and as she scrutinized the large hotel building against the backdrop of a vast gray sky and an unending open prairie, she began to weep, wondering what would happen to her in this place called America.

Coming out the door was a beautiful yellow-haired lady with piercing green eyes, wiping her hands on her apron.

"Hello, Alice," Dan called out. "Meet Ellen. She will be my partner for a while. Can we get her a bath and some clean clothes? By what I can smell coming from the kitchen, suppertime must be pretty near."

Alice laughed and waved her hand. "Hello, Danny. Come with me, Ellen, and I will take care of you. My name is Alice."

Soon, Ellen was resting in a tub of warm water in the large bathroom upstairs as Alice inventoried her clothing. "Tsk! You don't have much here, dear. I need to get you some things. Go ahead and soak awhile. I'll be right back."

Alice descended the stairway. Scribbling a list of items on a slip of hotel stationery, she called out to Pete, who was having coffee with Dan. "Pete, would you take this list and trot on over to the general store? These are girls' things I need for Ellen. Mrs. Swift will get them for you. Just have her put them on the hotel's tab."

Pete smiled at Dan, who smiled back. "'Trot on over,' she says," Pete chuckled. "Well, let's go. This will be good practice for the both of us."

Alice hurried up the stairs and helped Ellen out of the tub, wrapping her in a warm blanket until her clothing could arrive. "I have sent the men over to the store to fetch you some new clothes, honey. Just sit in that chair and keep warm by the stove."

Ellen said nothing but stared at Alice as she opened the drain cock on the tub. Weary, hungry, and not having had the companionship of other females for a very long time— being in fact accustomed to being treated like a scullery maid instead of someone's daughter—she was unable to contain herself any longer. She was starved for any hint or offering of love and affection. The tears began to flow from her eyes and find their way down her cheeks.

"Honey, what is it?" Alice asked in her soothing voice, going to her side and offering a warm embrace. "Are you ill?"

Ellen said nothing but laid her head against Alice's neck until the subtle drops of divine tranquilizer could accomplish their work and stay their own flow.

Finally, Ellen sat up and wiped her eyes, looking into Alice's face as she spoke, almost too weary to breathe.

"Ma'am, I'm so tired, and you remind me of my mother."

Alice's eyes sparkled as she pulled Ellen to herself and kissed her on her forehead. "I am glad that I remind you of your mother. I hope it helps," she said. "It would be a right honor to be the mother of a sweet girl like you. Now wait here. I hear the men downstairs, and I'm sure they have brought your new clothes."

* * *

Ellen finished a light supper and then asked to be excused. Alice showed her to a small room at the top of the stairs with a window facing the open prairie south of town. The young girl soon surrendered to her exhaustion and fell into a deep sleep. Tucking her in, Alice could not help but kiss her on the cheek, and quietly backing from the room, she closed the door.

"Folks?" Dan LaForge said, seated at the supper table with his friends. "I brought Ellen here for several reasons. I didn't want to drag a young girl around with me in this bitter weather as I worked my way back to Regina. I could have put her on the train in Canada, but I'm not sure of her family situation back east and need to sort it out. I thought if I brought her here, Alice and the other ladies could care for her. I know I'm asking a lot of my friends, but she's been treated for the most part like a bondservant for the last two years, and after her father's death, she needs to spend time with some genuine people. Could I leave her here with you until I can figure out what to do with her? If I can find some of her family willing to take her in, I'll come back and put her on the stage, and then send her home on the train from Havre or Chinook. Ontario is just across the river from Detroit, and it might be shorter than sending her back Canada way."

Alice answered first. "Danny, if Pete agrees, Ellen can stay with us as long as she likes. Speaking for my parents, we'd be happy to have her."

"Sounds good to me too, Dan," Pete said. "I think you did the compassionate thing, and I promise we won't try to make a Yankee out of her."

"I appreciate that, Pete," Dan said with a grin. "Tabulate her expenses while she is here; I'll settle up with you when I come back through to get her." He finished his cup of tea. "I'd like a room for tonight if you have one, and I'll leave early in the morning after breakfast. It's important that I make my report to my inspector as soon as I can."

Corporal LaForge stood up. "You may have to go easy with her at first, let her warm up to you. She's a little nervous about being here. Someone must have told her that Americans like to eat their young." He grinned, putting on his hat. "I must purchase supplies before I go and check on my horse and mule. I'll be back in a while. I need to speak with Ellen when she wakes and explain our little plan to her. It should be all right."

"Perhaps she might like to attend our school when she gets settled," Alice said. "Peggy Hamilton, Deputy Ben's wife, is our new schoolteacher from the state of Indiana. Ellen might find comfort speaking with her, since Peggy's mother is originally from Windsor."

"I'll take all the help I can get, my friends," Dan said, turning to exit the room. "By the way, how is Judith Farnsworth getting along?"

Alice raised her eyebrows. "That reminds me, Danny. She left a letter for you if you should come by." Alice walked to the clerk's desk and retrieved a cream-colored envelope from behind the counter. "She returned to Chicago about a month ago, pretty upset about Tom Brumett, I guess. There was no way for you to know."

Dan smiled a painful smile and nodded, inserting the envelope into the pocket of his tunic. "Thank you. I'll read it later," he said.

LaForge left the room, walking down the porch steps to the boardwalk to check on his animals at Hester's.

11
ARLISS RETURNS TO HAVRE

Taking advantage of the moderation in weather, Arliss readied his wagon and mules for the first trip of the year to fill supply orders from the town merchants. Never quite able to get over his wonder at the haste with which the temperatures could rise in the springtime during the Chinook winds as the steady westerly flow rolled across the prairies. Deep snows that seemed certain to cover and choke the landscape for months could vanish within days or sometimes in a few short hours.

Arliss intended to make at least several trips a month to the Hi-line in good weather. He hoped to well stock the warehouse he was leasing, ensuring no interruptions in supplies throughout the year. If he could then build up a mountain of coal and hundreds of gallons of kerosene, he would be close enough for some of the smaller towns like Turner and Hogeland, and the remote ranches and farms, to come to him instead of having to make the long journey to the rail line just for survival.

Arliss planned an early start in the morning before dawn. Peedy would not be coming this time but would remain under the watchful eyes of Alice and her folks at Granfield House so he could attend school.

The drive from Cantana to Havre by the route Arliss had chosen was every bit of fifty-plus miles. It was time-consuming and could be tedious, but there was no reason to risk damaging his wagon or injuring the mules by making haste. A new railroad spur would certainly be more efficient at hauling supplies, but in the process it would also put him out of business. Despite their friendship, Arliss secretly hoped all Pete's efforts to push for a spur wouldn't amount to anything. Many jobs, like the hauling of freight for small towns, existed only because nobody else wanted to take the time and effort to do the work.

* * *

Late in the evening of the second day, Arliss crossed the tracks near Havre and made his way to the livery to board his mules. Having had nothing but hardtack and dried beef to gnaw on, washed down with the sweetened cold coffee he kept in his canteen, he was anxious for some hot victuals and headed straight to Mrs. Hays's diner.

The place appeared to be empty and almost dark, telling him he had gotten there too late. Cupping his hands around his eyes against the glass of the door, he looked inside. He thought he could see a shadow passing back and forth against the dim lantern light at the back of the room. Perhaps he could prevail upon someone's good graces to sell him some bread and meat to take back with him to the wagon.

Knocking on the window glass, he saw the shadow stop and turn and walk to the door. "We are closed for the day, monsieur," a feminine voice rang out in a decidedly French accent.

Arliss pointed to his ear and shrugged his shoulders, pretending not to be able to hear her words. There was a pause, and he heard the lock click. The door opened.

"Go away! It is late, and we are closed," the woman said with a testy voice. As she attempted to secure the door again, Arliss stepped forward, blocking the door with his foot.

"Hold on, now. I am a friend. Mrs. Hays knows me. I was once a soldier from the fort. I've driven my wagon and team a long way. Can't I buy some bread and meat for my supper to tide me over?"

There was a long pause, and then the woman in the shadows invited him in, pointing to a seat in the corner. "Sit here and I will bring you something," she said, disappearing through the door to the kitchen.

Returning a few minutes later, the woman placed a large plate of food and biscuits in front of him, along with a large slab of apple pie on a saucer. She also carried a lamp, and after setting down the plate of food, she lit it with a match and turned up the flame. Arliss was surprised to see that it was the mysterious woman he had seen on the day he and Peedy stopped in for breakfast last autumn. He studied her face. She was fetching, with her shiny brown skin marked by smudges of flour on her chin and cheek. She wore a simple blue dress covered by a soiled apron that hung to her knees.

Smiling at him, she spoke. "Perhaps your stew will get cold if you don't eat it soon. Why do you stare at me so?"

"I've never seen anyone like you. You're as pretty as a jar of clover honey in the bright sunlight," Arliss said. He felt almost as if a spell had settled on him. "Won't you sit down and talk with me while I eat?"

The woman smiled again and pulled out the chair opposite Arliss. "You are certainly one most bold, monsieur. I was cleaning up the kitchen and making ready for the breakfast in the morning. Five minutes more and I would have been gone."

Arliss picked up his spoon and tasted of the beef stew, which was surprisingly warm and spicy. "I have learned that boldness serves me better these days. You have a French accent, but it's different from the French I've heard spoken by the Métis from Canada. What is your name?" he asked, sopping up some of the brown gravy with a warm biscuit.

"My name is Charlotte Bossard Pénot," she answered, subtly turning the lantern to get a better look at Arliss's face.

"So you are *Miss* Pénot, then?" Arliss asked.

"You may call me Charlotte. Miss Pénot is not necessary, and no, I am not married," Charlotte answered. "If my French accent sounds strange to your ears, it is because I am not from Canada. I was born in New Orleans near Metairie Ridge. I moved to Baton Rouge when I was a little girl. My people were French Acadians from Quebec. We are sometimes called Cajuns."

Arliss reached out and took her hand, turning her arm over to look at her skin. "Aren't Cajuns white? How is it you have brown skin?" he asked.

"Ooh, you are that bold, monsieur! My mother was Creole. Her father was a black man and her mother was French. Does it matter, big man?" He noted a sudden coolness in her tone. "It is like putting the cream with the coffee, no?"

Arliss's face turned grim. "You're not one of those voodoo women? You know—with charms and potions and amulets—reading chicken bones for money?" He searched her face for an honest answer. "I heard of it when I was growing up in Texas. My godly aunt was afraid to even speak of it."

Charlotte answered abruptly. "Certainly not, monsieur! I knew of such things, and they were not uncommon, but my parents were Christians. We were warned that such things are of the devil."

Arliss smiled. "I meant no insult, Charlotte. You come from such a different life . . . **thought I'd just ask."**

Arliss began to wipe the perspiration that had been forming on his hot face with his neckerchief. "May I have a glass of water, Charlotte? This stew is delicious, but I feel like I have bitten into a pepper sprout." He coughed hoarsely, growing more uncomfortable by the moment.

Charlotte chuckled. "Does the big man not like the stew? Have I not brought the spiciness of Cajun cooking to the blandness of the Montana prairies, yes?" She carried a pitcher of cool water to the table. Arliss took it from her with both hands and gulped it down.

Laughing at himself, his eyes watering, Arliss grinned at Charlotte. "I hope I'm able to sleep tonight. This stew is like eating fire!"

Charlotte grinned, handing him a clean towel. "It is good for your blood, monsieur. Perhaps you will not feel the need to drink so much whiskey after eating Charlotte's cooking? And you will sleep like the baby, I am sure."

Arliss broke up a biscuit and stirred it into his stew. "I never was much of a drinker, even in my younger days, but if I was, this stew would more than likely be a cure for it. May I ask how old you are, Charlotte?"

"You are so curious with the questions, monsieur. I am twenty-seven. Mrs. Hays hired me last summer to do her cooking, but soon I will be on my way to Seattle on the train—as you would say, to seek my fortune? Now what is your story, big man?"

Arliss cleaned the last of his food from his plate with a biscuit, washing it down with more water. "My story?" he chuckled. "I never thought of myself as having a story."

Arliss leaned back in his chair, staring at his new acquaintance. "I am from Texas, right next door to your Louisiana, and was raised by my aunt and uncle. I enlisted with the army at Fort Concho over San Angelo way with the 10th U.S. Cavalry, and then followed them north to Fort Assiniboine here in Montana. I finally left the military to be on my own. I guess I'm just a loner and wanderer at heart."

"I have settled down in Cantana just north of here. I do some work as a blacksmith and have started a business hauling freight. It isn't much now, but I've just begun. There are a lot of interesting things I've done too, but that is between me, my close friends, and God, I guess."

Charlotte grew still, and then standing, she said, "It is getting late, monsieur."

Arliss stood up, tossing a fifty-cent piece on the table. "My name is Arliss Moore if you are interested."

Charlotte smiled. "Pleased to meet you, Mr. Moore, and I do remember you when you came in last autumn with your little boy. Is he not your son?" She walked with him to the front door as she spoke.

"The boy's name is Peedy. I found him on the streets and have sort of taken him in," Arliss said, turning his hat around and around in his big hands.

"I suppose you and your wife will raise the young one to be a man, no?" she asked.

Arliss walked out the door, but before Charlotte could close and lock it again, he turned to answer her. "I will do my best to raise him to be a man—yes," he replied with a seriousness on his face and in his voice. "I don't have a wife to help me, so I will have to do it alone. Thank you, ma'am, for the meal and your kindness."

Arliss put on his hat and pinched the brim with a nod, then walked down the boardwalk to find his wagon.

12
THE MAN STEALERS

It was early morning Saturday, and Peggy Hamilton was busy in her small kitchen making a special dinner for herself and Ben to celebrate his birthday. She had just come back from Swift's general store with a new leather belt she had purchased for him as a gift.

Perhaps it is not such a special gift, she thought, wishing she could have bought him a new shiny watch or a pair of boots. But the Hamilton's, with their Hoosier upbringing, had a frugal, practical bend of mind. Ben would no doubt appreciate the value of the belt.

From a brown paper package, Peggy removed a large roasting hen freshly dressed that morning by Mr. Swift and placed it in a porcelain baking pan. Rubbing it all over with soft butter, she filled the cavity with bread stuffing mixed with sage, onion and lovage leaves, an herb from her window sill garden that tasted like celery. Then, setting the bird on a bed of carrots, parsnips, and potatoes to roast, she set the pan in a slow oven to gently bake all morning in

103

time for the dinner meal.

Ben was not partial to cake, so for dessert, Peggy baked a simple custard pie made of eggs, sugar, vanilla bean, cornmeal, and a mixture of cream and canned milk. Sometimes called *sugar pie* by the old-timers, it was an easy concoction to make, and it was satisfying of a person's cravings for something sweet.

It was nearing the time Ben was expected home for dinner. Peggy changed into her new dress as a surprise. It was made of light green cloth with white trimmings, Ben's favorite color combination.

As she watched the time, the clock struck out the hour . . . but then it was ten after, and now the half-hour. Perhaps Ben was delayed with the affairs of his job at the marshal's office.

It being Saturday, Pete might not be there to spell him so he can come to dinner, Peggy pondered. But finally, it was one o'clock, and Peggy's pondering had become concern. She quickly pulled her shawl over her shoulders and headed down the boardwalk to the marshal's office. The streets were deserted except for the presence of Arliss Moore, who was mending a leather harness in front of Hester's livery. Rushing up to the marshal's office, Peggy readied to rap on the door but stopped, struggling to understand what she was seeing.

There, fastened to the heavy door at a tall man's eye level, was a deputy's badge, secured in place by what appeared to be a brand new railroad spike, driven straight through its center.

Peggy easily recognized the scratches and a small dent on one of the star points. It belonged to Ben.

Turning on her heels, she shouted to Arliss Moore, who immediately came running to her side. Pausing for a moment to gaze at that which was fastened to the marshal's door, he pushed the door open. There were chairs overturned and items strewn about the room, indicating that quite a struggle had taken place. The back door was wide open, but Ben was not there.

Whatever had happened, Ben had not gone along with it without a fight.

* * *

Within the hour, Pete had made ready to begin his search for Ben. As he stood beside Sadie loading his Winchester saddle rifle, Arliss Moore approached.

"Pete, I made a quick circle of the town and located some fresh tracks headed south-southwest," he said. "Looks to be at least three riders."

Pete nodded. "Thanks. Ben's horse is still here, so whoever they are must have brought one for him to ride. I asked around town to find out if anyone saw anything. Macgregor at the Red Angus told me a couple of men had been asking for directions to Havre. He said they were loud and boisterous, almost on purpose, like they wanted everyone in the saloon to hear them. He'd never seen them before, but they made it clear they were on their way to the train station in Havre." Pete checked Sadie's feet, nearly ready to go.

"How's Peggy holding out?" Arliss asked.

"Alice and Ellen are over there with her now. I don't have to tell you, Arliss, how this eats me up inside. I touted Cantana as a nice friendly town to get Ben to take the job as deputy. How can I ever atone for this if Ben is hurt or worse?"

Arliss shook his head. "It's no different than someone who signs up to join the army. When you pin on a badge, you must know that it could one day end badly. Ben is no novice. He knew it was a dangerous job when he took it."

Arliss put his big hand on Pete's shoulder. "And Pete, you understand what this is all about, don't you? Someone in the railroad is giving you back your own for stirring up a nest of hornets about that spur. When you sent those letters to the newspapers, you must have crossed the wrong people at headquarters in Minnesota. You made one of the most important, powerful men in America and the Great Northern Railway look bad in front of the whole country. And that railroad spike used to nail Ben's badge to the door—that's as clear a message as you can get. Likely they are the ones who took Ben, so we have to be careful that we're not playing right into their hands."

"How is that, Arliss?" Pete asked.

"They took Ben to get at you, to draw you out of town, and you're doing exactly what they expected you'd do," Arliss answered. "If they get you out on that open prairie alone, they will shoot you for sure!"

"So what am I supposed to do? I can't let them, whoever they are, think they have me and do nothing. I have to find Ben and save him if I can," Pete said. "Even if it means riding into a trap." He reached up and gripped his saddle horn.

Arliss spoke. "Wait, Pete. Let's talk. You remember our fight in the Bear Paws? We were outnumbered and outgunned, so we had to find a way to turn it around and make sure the advantage was ours. It's the same here with this. We know these people are watching and expecting you to go out all half-cocked. You are the marshal, and Ben's your friend and deputy, so they expect you to be fueled with revenge, and maybe not thinking straight. But one thing is clear to me: you can be assured that they will wait and dry-gulch you as soon as you get outside of town."

Pete slid his rifle into its saddle boot. "So are you saying I don't have a chance?"

"I'm saying that you need a plan. Let's study this thing. I have a feeling that Ben will not be harmed as long as you stay alive. But once they get to you, they will kill him. Now, like I told you, I've checked, and there are several sets of tracks leading directly southwest out of town. But I think it's a ruse. Those men earlier today who ran their mouths in Macgregor's saloon wanted to make awful sure you got the message that they would be heading in the direction of Havre so you would follow them there. I think they are the same people who kidnapped Ben, and they are going to wait southwest of town between here and Havre, hiding along some coulee and setting you up for an ambush. I would not be surprised if they were keeping Ben with them close by so they can finish him off after they get you."

"You paint a glum picture, my friend," Pete said. "Okay, Sergeant Moore, what's the plan?"

"Here's what we do, Pete. Let's assume they will be watching for you. Go ahead and start out southwest in the direction of Havre. I will make a wide circle to the east and follow you on your left flank at a distance. If I can spot them first, I may have a good chance to get off a couple of lucky shots. I have a new rifle I got from a friend at Fort Assiniboine, a .30–40 Krag; it shoots flat, and the gunpowder it uses barely gives off any smoke, so it shouldn't draw too much attention. Our advantage is that they will be looking for you to be alone and not expecting me to be stalking them from afar. Our disadvantage is that they might have other men lurking along the way, waiting to get at you from several different angles. Anywise, they will kill Ben if we don't get to them first."

"All right, Buffalo Soldier," Pete said, smiling, remembering the precision with which Arliss had planned and carried out the attack on the outlaws in the Bear Paw Mountains several years ago. "Let's do this thing. Grab your rifle and let's go. But I hope you see them before they see me."

Pete secured the rope that hung from his saddle. He grew thoughtful. "Arliss, why are you suddenly so willing to help Ben? You hardly know the man."

Arliss smiled. "The pitiful look on Peggy Hamilton's face, for one. Another is that I was working at Hester's a few days ago and noticed Peedy walking this way down the boardwalk all alone. As usual, his shoestrings were untied and dragging behind him; I could see them even from where I was standing. Just then, Ben stepped out of Swift's store and picked Peedy up and set him on a bench. Ben tied both of his shoes, wiped his nose with his own handkerchief, and gave him a sugar-stick from his pocket. That's all."

Pete nodded and smiled. "So—let me deputize you to make it all official."

Arliss was grim. "No. What I may have to do, I don't want to do with a badge on. So far, there's a shine still on your badge. Keep it that way—nice and clean. It'll be better if you follow your way and I follow mine."

Pete didn't push the matter. Arliss knew what he was doing, and to get Ben back without harm, extraordinary things might have to be done. It might be best if Pete didn't officially know what that might mean.

Arliss saddled his horse as Pete and Sadie headed southward out of town. He got his new rifle from the freight office, and just in case, packed enough grub to tide him over for several days. Quickly stopping by Granfield House on his way out of town, he left word for Alice to watch over Peedy until he returned.

Immediately riding east of town, Arliss worked on a strategy in his head that he hoped would bring Ben home safely and keep his friend Pete Randers out of hot water.

13
THE MAN HUNTERS

Taking a gulp from his canteen, Pete replaced the stopper, tamping it closed with his fist and draping the strap over his saddle horn. Scanning the horizon, he occasionally glanced down to follow the faint hoof marks and laid-over grasses in his path.

Until he saw something different.

Stopping, he quickly dismounted for a closer look. There in the sand were several well-defined shoe marks, distinctly from three different horses. It appeared that Ben with his two kidnappers had come this way. Pete's heart began to pound as he pressed on.

Riding Sadie across the plain, searching each coulee to follow the tracks, he became increasingly aware of the sun's arc, plunging to the horizon like a bright yellow comet across the western sky. Pete imagined that he should have already made contact with those men waiting to intercept him. He needed for it to happen soon, because darkness without pity was about to add itself to the equation.

Riding up the fairly steep side of a small hill to get a better look around him, he flushed a small herd of antelope. Almost instantly, a shot rang out from the distance.

What nut would be shooting at those pronghorns? was his first thought. Several more shots rang out, and the dust at Sadie's feet exploded. Pete dug his heels into her sides and she reared up. As he heard the third shot, he felt Sadie tremble and collapse under her own weight.

The stranger or strangers in the impending dusk had shot his beloved horse.

Sadie struggled to get up as Pete squirmed to pull his leg out from under her. Freeing himself, he ran his hand over the bloody wetness along her withers and determined that she had been shot somewhere in the neck, perhaps through the spine, and was gasping for air. The nearness of the hit to his saddle told him the shot was probably meant for him.

Pete felt his eyes well up with moisture as he hugged Sadie's head and spoke softly into her ear. Slowly pulling his revolver, he held it against her forehead and cocked the hammer. He said goodbye and kissed her eye, pulling the trigger.

Sadie's body shuddered and then was silent and still, and mercifully she felt no more pain.

Another rifle slug struck Sadie's lifeless form. Pete would have to postpone his grieving. He could hear several more shots in the distance from another location, but the trajectory was way off . . . as if the second shooter was trying to miss him on purpose.

As he waited silently in the low light of the prairie evening, the shooting ceased. Perhaps the shooter figured his job was done and had fled to get away, perhaps with Ben, wounded or dead. Or were they still out there? Waiting? Watching?

Pete dug into his pocket. Unclasping his knife, he cut off a few strands of mane from Sadie's neck and stuffed them into his shirt pocket as a remembrance. Rubbing her on the bridge of her nose one last time, Pete took his Winchester, bedroll, canteen, and war bags and rolled down the hill into the darkness and waited, his shirt soaked with Sadie's blood.

He tried to discern what had happened. And where was Arliss? Had they got him too? Was he lying out there somewhere bleeding to death?

Pete crawled across the prairie on his belly as the last colors of the horizon faded into twilight, thankful there was darkness to hide his escape. If he got out of this predicament, he would retrieve his saddle later and bury Sadie where she lay. Listening carefully for a while, he heard no more shots and perceived that he was alone. Arliss's instincts had been right as usual. Storing up all the righteous anger his heart would hold, Pete made his vow:

I'll meet up with them again real soon and see them swingin' from a rope!

Finally, with only starlight as his guide, Pete felt confident enough to put a few miles between him and where Sadie lay. There were no ranches nearby, so borrowing a fresh horse was not an option.

He did not know if the scoundrels who had fired at him and killed Sadie might still be out there, still tracking him in the dark, so he had to set up a cold camp, sitting in the darkness alone with no fire or hot food. Pete spread out his bedroll and sat down, taking a bite of raw bacon from his war bags and washing down the greasy, congealed mush with cold water. He would get a few hours' sleep and head back to Cantana in the morning to begin his search all over again.

* * *

Earlier that day . . .

The sun was in Arliss's eyes as he constantly scanned the coulees and grasses in the distance and along the horizon for any sign of movement. He watched and followed Pete from as far away as he dared. He could tell that Pete was being diligent, but how much can you do when someone is hiding along the ground with an assassin's heart, watching and waiting for you to present yourself as an oblivious target?

Arliss watched Pete as he suddenly turned and rode up the side of a steep hill just as a shot rang out from somewhere. A herd of antelope scattered and fled in several directions as more shots could be heard, and then to his horror, Pete's beautiful horse fell underneath him. Arliss could not tell if Pete had been hit, but he heard the single shot from a revolver and then could see no more movement.

And then Arliss saw them: two men with rifles lying prone along the ridge of the same coulee, shooting in Pete's direction. Quickly dismounting his old cavalry horse, trained to stand absolutely still under fire, Arliss yanked his Krag rifle from the saddle boot. Adjusting the rifle's sight and taking careful aim at one of the men, he held his breath and fired. The man slumped over his rifle and did not move again. The second man appeared to be shooting wildly, but not in Pete's direction. Arliss began to fire at him, but this time, he purposely hit the ground near him until the man stood up with his hands raised high above his head.

Taking a chance that the man was alone and had sincerely given up, Arliss remounted his horse and raced to his location. When he arrived, he could see that the first man was dead. The second man, with hands to the sky, shouted out to Arliss not to shoot him.

Seeing no one else, Arliss dismounted. He held the barrel of his rifle against the man's chest and spoke softly, almost in a whisper. "Where is the deputy?"

The man shook his head. Arliss cycled the action on his rifle and this time, placed the barrel against the man's forehead.

"He's east of here in the direction of Hogeland, tied up in an old soddy—no one is there with him," the man cried out.

"One more question and one more breath and your answer better make me happy. Is the deputy hurt?" Arliss asked. As the man shied away from giving his answer, Arliss knocked the end of his rifle barrel against the man's temple. The shooter crumpled to his feet as if someone had pulled the ground out from under him. "He's not hurt, I tell ya! He's not hurt. Please don't hit me again!"

Arliss composed himself and tied the man's hands tightly behind him. Finding three horses hidden a short distance away in a deep coulee, he helped the man to his saddle.

"As long as you're not lying to me, we'll get along just fine," Arliss growled. "But if I find the deputy has been hurt or is dead, or if someone is there waiting for us, this will be your last day on earth." Arliss pulled the man's horse close to his. "And you're not going to die as easy as your friend back there. Let's go!"

Arliss made his way in the almost dark prairie to where he had last seen Pete. Finding Sadie's lifeless body, he gave his head a shake, observing how Pete had administered a final act of love to his suffering friend. He circled the area but could not find Pete. He figured his friend might be miles away by now, hunkered down somewhere awaiting the morning light so he could safely make his way back to town.

Finally, Arliss had to leave and find Ben, just in case there were more cutthroats waiting to give him trouble.

And as he made very clear to the man on the horse beside him, if he found Ben dead or beat up, or more railroad toadies there waiting—Arliss was not Pete. He would surely save the judge and jury the time and expense of a trial, letting the prairie swallow up and digest what was left of them all.

* * *

As Arliss neared the place, it started to drizzle. The man on the horse next to him spoke. "It's straight up ahead. See that clump of brush and that rock? The soddy is just to the left of the rock."

Arliss stopped and pulled the man down off his horse, checking the length of rope that held his hands. "Is that too tight for you?" Arliss asked.

The man looked up at him, surprised. "No, its fine," he muttered.

Arliss uncorked his canteen and took a long drink. Wiping the spout with his sleeve, he let the thirsty man drink freely. "I'm going to untie your hands so you can take

117

care of your personal business, but you understand that if you try anything funny, I'll shoot you, right?"

The man cracked a slight smile at the corner of his mouth as Arliss undid his hands. "I'll give you one more chance to fess up and change your story," Arliss told him. "If there's someone up there waiting for us, you will be the first one I shoot."

The man grunted. "No, it's the way I said—the deputy is alone."

Arliss took his first deliberate look at the man before him. He looked pitiful, with a swollen eye and a bloody gash above his ear . . . really only a boy in his late teens whom bad relatives or bad companions had influenced. Arliss sensed he wasn't really up to an outlaw's life, and he was probably too scared to lie. How easily it could have been this lad that Arliss had shot back there.

"If I find Deputy Hamilton alive and well and no other jackals lurking about, I'll make us some breakfast and fix that gash on your head," Arliss said, retying the young man's hands and helping him to his horse. The boy didn't respond.

As the two men approached the spot, Arliss dismounted with his rifle, and putting it to his shoulder, he shouted, "Throw down your guns and come out of there. I'm well armed and can drop you before you get through the door!"

Arliss waited and then repeated his orders, but all was

quiet. Cautiously approaching the doorway, which was only a piece of tattered canvas stretched across the entrance, he stood aside and carefully pulled it open. It was dark and dirty, but someone was definitely in there. Carefully breaching the space, Arliss soon reemerged with a man, tied and gagged. It was Ben.

Arliss pulled the gag from Ben's mouth and commenced to cutting him free. Ben smiled but didn't speak, too dry-mouthed and weary for unnecessary words. Turning to face his young prisoner behind him on the horse, Arliss spoke. "Well, boy, it appears you told me the truth. He doesn't look any worse for the wear."

Giving Ben a long draft from his canteen, Arliss helped him to the empty horse belonging to the dead man they'd left behind in the prairie grass.

"Let's head out. I still don't trust this place," Arliss said. The three men started north toward Cantana with one riderless horse trailing behind.

14

THE NEED TO SORT THINGS OUT

Late in the afternoon, one of the local farmers who managed to coexist among the cattle ranchers rode into town with his buckboard, stopping in front of the marshal's office. With a grin, the driver turned in his seat and reaching behind him, shook the sleeping man who lay there.

"Marshal Randers? Wake up, Marshal! We're here!" Pete stirred from his place where he had been napping among the sun-warmed feed sacks in the back of the wagon. Blinking his eyes, he grabbed his rifle and other things and slid off the tailgate. "Thanks Jim," he shouted to the farmer and nodded. The farmer had found him walking along the prairie toward the town and saved him some time and wear besides.

Limping, Pete made his way over to see Bill Hester, who was busy at his forge making nails.

"Bill, I need to borrow a good horse and saddle," he said. "I also got another problem."

The two men walked inside the livery out of the street. Pete grimaced. "I rolled over a cactus patch in the dark last night. Could you help me get shed of these needles? I feel like a pin cushion."

Bill Hester chuckled. "It happens, doesn't it? Wish I had a dollar for every time I've had to pick cactus spines from a cowboy's butt. You'll live, though."

Sore and slightly red-faced, Pete walked across the street to his office with his borrowed horse and saddle, replenished supplies, and extra boxes of 44s for his revolver and rifle. He opened the door sadly, noting the office was still in disarray from the struggle that had occurred between Ben and his captors. He picked up his chair and set it behind his desk. His coffeepot had been flattened in the melee. *Maybe Alice has an old one I can borrow.*

Walking down the street to speak with Peggy Hamilton, he found that she was staying at Granfield House for the time being. There was no news of Arliss Moore.

Pete headed over to the hotel to see Alice and check on Peggy. Tying his horse to the porch rail, he hurried up the steps and through the front door. Alice was busy at the clerk's desk, a sight for sore eyes.

Pete was tired, hungry, frustrated, and sad about Sadie . . . and on top of that a little embarrassed. He looked forward to Alice's embrace, smelling her perfume and being on the receiving end of her kisses and encouragement.

He began to relate to her what had happened and what

he was about to do, but instead of throwing her arms around his neck and making him feel that special way that only she could, Alice reared up with a fiery temper he had not seen in her before.

"I don't want you to go," she said flatly. "Peter, you're trying to do the impossible again, and all by yourself. Why don't you contact the U.S. marshal or the county sheriff?" Her voice rose almost to a shout. "This is just like when you headed off to the Bear Paws after those missionaries. It's just a miracle you weren't killed!"

Pete could not have been caught more off guard had he awakened that morning to find his boots nailed to the floor. Alice was truly angry and upset—a side of her he had never seen before.

"Alice, are you saying you don't expect me to do my job? To go after Ben and them that took him?" he said after taking a few thought-gathering moments. "It would take at least a week to find the marshal and get hold of the sheriff at Fort Benton. Besides, it's my job, not theirs."

Alice didn't seem to hear his words. "I'm tired of worrying about you, Pete, wondering what crazy thing will come along and impose itself upon you next. I want to get married and have a life now, not go on like this waiting for you to be killed."

Alice began to weep. "Perhaps I had not realized that the hazards of your job would always be there, calling upon you to face some unexpected menace and maybe death. You put off our wedding so you could adjust to your new job, then it was to find the right man to be your deputy. Now you have him, and he is not here when you need him!"

Pete furrowed his brow and struck back. "That's not fair, Alice, and it doesn't make any sense! Ben didn't kidnap himself, did he? And do you expect me to run everything I do past you for approval? I'm the marshal, and this is my job, not yours."

Pete looked into Alice's eyes, and it was as if he could feel the great wedge being driven between them. Putting his hat on, he turned to leave. "If this is the way it is with us, then maybe it's for the best we didn't get hitched before now. Or maybe ever."

Pete stepped to the edge of the porch, untied his horse and quickly swung his leg over the saddle, bumping his heels against the horse's sides. Startled, she reared up and headed south of town in the direction he hoped would lead him to his deputy, Ben Hamilton, and his friend Arliss Moore.

* * *

Peggy Hamilton sat on the back porch of Granfield House, bewildered, not knowing what to do. Ben had been a lawman for years, and this wasn't the first time she had waited alone for him to come back, wondering if something had happened when he was late coming home. She was supposed to be an old hand at this, but this was different — Ben had been kidnapped.

They'd come west mostly for her sake, she knew that. Ben had really wanted to take that job as chief of police back in Indiana. But he'd given it up to have this adventure with her, and secretly, she had been glad when Pete asked him to be his deputy. She could tell he really wanted to wear a badge and gun again. The job was his first love; she knew it was what he wanted to do. Now she could only wait and watch, rocking on the porch and sipping tea.

She placed her hand on her waist, wondering in her heart if the child she was carrying would ever get to see its papa.

Alice came out and moved another rocker next to Peg. Together they sat in silence, unsure of anything they could say to each other that would help.

"Alice?" Peg finally said. "I heard what you said to Pete. I didn't mean to eavesdrop, but I had just walked in while you were talking."

Alice was instantly mortified. "Peg, I'm so sorry. I didn't mean what I said. I was just so upset. It was an unkind and unfair thing to say." She took Peggy's hand in hers. "But Pete was right. It is his job. He was a marshal long before we met and will always be one, I suppose. I was wrong to interfere. He came to me for comfort, and I sent him out of here all twisted up inside. And said unkind things about your husband as well. Peg? Forgive me?"

Peggy smiled, but before she could answer, she froze, squeezing Alice's hand. "Alice, look!" she shouted, pointing out over the prairie. In the faint distance, they could barely make out three riders and an empty horse heading into town.

"Could it be?" Peggy asked with an almost prayerful tremble and pleading in her voice.

As the riders came closer into view, the women could make out Arliss and Ben. The third man, with his hands tied, they had not seen before. The empty horse certainly had its own story, which they would doubtless soon discover.

Rushing off the porch, Peggy ran to her husband, who had just slid off his horse to the ground. Embracing, Peggy wept, whispering in her heart, *I've got him back one more time! Thank you, Lord Jesus!*

"Has Pete been here?" Arliss asked.

"Yes," Alice answered. "He came in about an hour ago and got provisioned up and lit out again south of town, looking for you and Ben."

"Ben?" Arliss shouted orders, as was his way when he took charge. "Lock up our boy here. I'm going after Pete alone."

He leaned forward. "Alice, did Pete tell you about Sadie?"

Alice shook her head. "What?"

"The men that took Ben shot Sadie out from under him.

She's lying out there on the prairie south of town. I'm surprised he didn't tell you. Well, I'm off," he said, turning his horse and galloping away.

Alice watched Arliss disappear in the distance. Her eyes filled with tears once again. *Pete wanted to tell me, but I didn't give him much of a chance*, she thought.

* * *

As a light rain began to blow over the prairie from low hanging clouds all gray and black, Arliss put up his collar and pulled his hat down to cover his face. He had an idea where Pete might be, and when he finally caught up with him, he was standing beside Sadie's remains. Arliss whistled as he approached so as not to startle Pete.

"Ho Marshal!" he said, dismounting his horse. Being an old cavalryman himself, Arliss understood just how attached one could get to a faithful horse. But he also knew there was little he could say that would make a difference now. Standing quietly next to his friend would have to be enough.

Finally, breaking the silence, Arliss spoke. "Ben is safe with a few bumps and bruises; the second culprit is locked up in your jail. Sorry I had to kill the other guy . . . had no choice. He's layin' that way about a hundred and fifty yards." Arliss pointed southward.

Pete turned and removed the shovel attached to his

saddle. "Sorry for what?" he said bluntly, as he began to dig the large deep hole he'd need for the horse's body.

"When I'm done with Sadie, we can bury our friend over there too, if the coyotes haven't gotten to him first."

* * *

Ben took up his duties as deputy marshal, seeming to relish his job even more than before. Peggy was again able to turn her thoughts to her students, and a visiting army doctor who came through town with a troop on the way to Fort Assiniboine set up a day clinic at Granfield House for the people of Cantana. With a smile, he cheerfully told her that he could find no reason for her not to expect a normal birth.

An investigation conducted by the U.S. marshal regarding Ben's kidnapping and the attempted murder of Pete confirmed their suspicions. Pete's letters to the newspapers and the railroad had caught the attention of someone in the railroad hierarchy who had decided to quietly resolve the matter himself by hiring a gunman to silence the young marshal. Pete was further surprised to learn that the identity of this gunman was Ronald Guidice, the failed applicant for deputy marshal he had interviewed that day in the town of Chinook, being also the cowboy Arliss had shot out on the prairie. Bitter over his rejection by Pete, he'd been an easy, willing participant, eager to do the dirty work of a railroad official seeking to discourage an enthusiastic, civic-minded town marshal.

It had not yet been determined if it was the official's intention to have murder done or if Mr. Guidice had made that decision himself. They would never know the gunman's complete side of the story, because Arliss had decided the matter himself that day out on the prairie.

The way of transgressors is hard, Pete thought, remembering the Scripture verse. *And sometimes deeds come with their own built-in judgment and justice, often from outside the courtroom and apart from the gallows.*

Pete sent Guidice's young partner to Havre for trial. Arliss and Ben would be there to testify on the young man's behalf—that he had been cooperative and instrumental in finding Ben alive and unharmed. Ben revealed that Guidice had wanted to kill him then and there, but the young man talked him out of it, convincing him that a live deputy might be of better use to them as a chip to bargain with later on. Arliss also believed that the young man had purposely made his shots go wild to avoid hitting Pete. It was hoped that he might get a prison sentence instead of a rope, and having been extended mercy, perhaps someday might be returned to a more honest and honorable existence in Montana's cattle country.

* * *

Pete stood with his hat in his hand inside the half-acre of

yellow grass that was the Cantana Cemetery. He often came here when he needed to brood. Walking between the stone markers and the weathered wooden crosses, he recounted the names and lives of the people he had known well who were buried here amidst others from the town's early days, whose lives and deaths were but a mystery.

Doc Blake, the old town doctor, was here. A slain Mountie and his dog lay there, near a few outlaws who had crossed swords with Marshal Brenton to their regret. Several Chinese who had come to Cantana to start new lives and new businesses lay here also. Some, having lost their own due to prejudice and others for reasons known only to themselves, had failed to escape the undertaker's cabinetmaker.

Pete, with a thought to the practical, noted how few usable plots were left within the wrought-iron enclosure. *Soon a fence will have to come down to make room for more graves*, he thought. It was only by God's grace they hadn't been needed just a few weeks ago.

Pete slapped the dust from his hat several times, disappointed with himself. Instead of following in Marshal Brenton's footsteps, endeavoring to be the best lawman he could, he had meddled in politics, got his deputy kidnapped and almost killed, and probably ruined Cantana's chances for survival forever. And now he had lost the regard and respect of his girl, Alice, someone he'd thought would have never left his side.

Walking back to his office, he thought, *I need time to sort things out.*

15
THE RAILROAD TAKES IT PERSONAL

Pete was glad and even proud that Ben had weathered the storm because in his heart, he had entertained a notion in passing that his new deputy might be a weak easterner and resign. But Ben and Peggy Hamilton were tough Hoosiers of pure pioneer stock, and they took all that life could throw at them in stride. Peggy continued her duties as schoolteacher, stopping off at the marshal's office frequently during the day to tap on the window and smile at her husband. Pete was gratified that he had chosen the right man and woman for the job, thinking back on the day he happened upon the two gophers on the open prairie.

It was midafternoon, and the every-other-week stage had arrived in Cantana amidst a steady rain that converted the roads and Main Street into a rutted muddy morass. Pete left the dry, warm fire of the marshal's office to get the mailbag and take it over to Granfield House.

Alice met him at the clerk's desk. His somewhat short, formal greeting and her cool response showed that not much had changed since their brouhaha over Pete's decision to go after Ben alone. He understood her concern for his safety, but he could not forgive her interfering and questioning his duty and responsibility.

Not only that, but he was more hurt than he wanted to admit. Pete had wanted to tell Alice about Sadie's death and what it meant to him, but he'd never gotten the chance. Perhaps he'd assumed all along that Alice would be another Melinda Brenton. She and his mentor had been his foster parents in his youth, and he held Melinda up as the ideal of a marshal's wife. Alice had unknowingly violated and contaminated that image, and Pete did not know how or if he could ever get around it. How this would all end, surely neither of them had a clue.

As Pete waited for Alice to finish sorting the mail, she silently slid a letter addressed to him across the counter. He took it and sat down in one of the lobby chairs, gazing at the printing along the seal flap: *Great Northern Railway.*

Now what? Pete thought, opening the envelope with his pocket knife. He unfolded the letter written on elegant stationery. Its message was short and sweet. A meeting had been requested between himself and some corporate official with the Great Northern, to take place at Havre in two weeks' time. *Please confirm* was scribbled across the bottom of the page in someone's cursive hand and underlined twice.

Pete stood up and hurried to the clerk's desk to write a

quick note of response. He handed it to Alice, asking her if she would make sure it went out with the stage that would be leaving soon. He emphasized how important it was, and Alice nodded and uttered a weak "yes" under her breath.

Sadly, those words were the most they had spoken to each other in weeks.

* * *

Pete was only a mile from Havre, riding a buckboard into town to keep his appointment with the railroad. He had only ridden wagons and borrowed horses since the death of Sadie, and only when absolutely necessary. His sorrow had taken him too far and he needed to get over it and choose a new horse. Had things been different, Alice would have noticed this and tenderly spoken to him about it.

It was close to noon, and his mind wandered a bit as he remembered passing through the Hi-line several years earlier during that bitter winter to find the Farnsworth's, the faithful missionaries to the Nez Perce Indians who had been murdered by wicked men in their pursuit of gold. Time had moved on since then, and all of these experiences had grown him a much thicker hide. Now he was marshal, and in less than an hour he would be meeting with an important man to ask him to his face to keep the company's word to a small, insignificant town on the northernmost border of Montana. Pete would soon discover if any of the resulting bloodshed and trouble of the last few months had come close to being worth it.

Pete crossed the tracks and headed into town to the Havre station. There on a side track was a large shiny private car that had been, no doubt, well appointed to serve its master. Several men milled around outside it, some dressed in their business best with shiny top hats and coats with fur collars, while others washed the windows and saw to the restocking of food and supplies. Without fanfare, Pete dismounted the buckboard and made his way to the door of the train car. Smoke and heat poured from the several chimneys on the roof. One of the men standing guard near the doorway asked him his name and told him that he was expected, gesturing for him to take the steps leading to the bowels of the car.

As Pete made his way down a short hallway, he was impressed by how dark it was inside. All the car's curtains of forest green were drawn but one, letting only a little light in from outside. Waiting for his eyes to adjust, he soon became aware of the elegant, plush furnishings and a man seated at a comfortable table with overstuffed leather chairs on either side of him. The man smiled at Pete.

"Come in. Come in, sir. Won't you have a seat here next me, Marshal? John will help you with your coat. I hope it's not too warm in here for you. There is a decided chill in the air, so I had John make up the fire. Before we talk, I thought we might have dinner together. You must have an appetite after driving all that way."

Pete responded to the man's cordiality by removing his hat and coat and handing it to the older black man dressed in a white jacket standing beside him. Pete smiled, nodded, and took his seat, wondering to himself about the identity of the obviously important man seated on the throne-like chair before him. He had expected to meet with one of the railroad's flunkies but could this be Mr. Hill himself?

"Marshal Randers, may I get you a cup of coffee or tea? I understand you are not a drinking man," the man asked.

"Coffee would be fine, sir. Thank you," Pete responded, curious that the man knew of his personal habits.

As he looked about at all the evidence of privilege and affluence, it was clear to Pete that he was out of his element and his station.

Noticing the many preserved animal heads mounted along the walls, he focused on that of a large timber wolf grinning down at him from over a blazing stove in one of the corners. His mind raced back to the near-deadly wolf attack he had suffered around the campfire in the Bear Paws several years previous. He wondered if this so-called great man who sat before him, if that great man he be, had ever considered the lives and experiences of the real people affected by the orders routinely divvied out by him.

As if he had read Pete's thoughts, the man spoke. "My name is Hill. Perhaps you are surprised that I would come myself? I imagined that you probably had enough of dealing with those in my organization who have purported to speak for me. My name and my word are at stake here. So with all that has happened, I had a keen desire to meet with you face to face."

Pete took a sip from his cup, which appeared to be made of the finest china. Though he tried not to stare, he was curious about the man who sat before him. Mr. Hill appeared to be about sixty years old. He was balding, with gray hair, mustache, and beard. Dressed in a three-piece suit, he had the look of one who possessed wealth but did not seem to be conscious of it nor feel a need to flaunt it.

The two men casually engaged in small talk about Montana, the prairie and its people, and what it was like to be a marshal. Soon, a cart was rolled up to their table by John, who was obviously employed to care for the personal needs of the mysterious Mr. Hill seated in the shadows, known to America as "the Empire Builder."

"I hope you like roast pheasant, Marshal. Done right, there is nothing that is its equal. Please eat hearty. I prefer not to eat alone," Mr. Hill said cheerfully. Pete smiled and served himself.

After a dessert of apple cobbler and ice cream, fresh coffee was served, and the two men again faced each other. Pete had enjoyed this momentary taste of luxury and brush with the elite, but being a cowboy at heart, he was anxious to get on with it . . . feeling perhaps that the man might be buttering him up so he could let him down easy.

"Marshal Randers, I'm sure you have heard things about me," Mr. Hill said, smiling. "Let me begin by expressing my apologies for the way you and your deputy were treated. I assure you that I knew nothing of this until the end, and those in my organization who were responsible will pay for their crimes. Regardless of what you may have heard, I am not an evil robber baron. That is not how I care to conduct business, and I take things like this very personally. I never received any correspondence regarding your requests, and it is those matters that I am here to discuss."

"Sir, let me cut through the smoke. Are we going to get our spur?" Pete interrupted.

The man chuckled. "I have a great deal of respect for you, Marshal. You don't seem to be the type who lets anyone back him down. Let me stop yammering and get to the point. I looked into your proposal for a spur to be built from the nearest depot on what is called the Hi-line to the border of Canada, which would be at a minimum about thirty miles. A spur of that length would almost be a railroad unto itself, all to service one remote town with no other destinations beyond it. It just isn't close to being feasible from a business point of view. I understand your reasoning—that prosperity and growth often follow the tracks—but in this case I believe it would be excess, and not the most efficient way to help your town. The promise by the railroad to build a spur was based upon an expectation

137

that Cantana would become a great center of commerce. That did not happen. A spur built now would do nothing to help the town, and I believe, would hurt it in the end."

Pete was crestfallen, knowing now that all of his efforts had been in vain. Sensing that the other foot was about to fall, he asked John, who was standing nearby, for his hat and coat. He stood up to depart when Mr. Hill raised his hand and asked him not to go.

"Let me finish, sir. I have an alternate proposal I would like to discuss," he said, motioning for Pete to retake his seat. "Now, here is what the railroad is willing to do. We will first restore the telegraph line from Chinook to Cantana and pay to have it maintained. Secondly, I will sign a pledge to pay the future expenses of running telephone and electrical wires to Cantana when they become available to this part of Montana. Also, we will build and improve a roadway leading to Cantana, which should make it easier for the stage and freight wagons to get there and back. That will put your town years ahead of other places. Will you accept my offer?"

Pete was quiet, thinking about what he had just heard. "It seems I have no other choice," he said finally, smarting a bit from the news that the spur was now off the table for good.

"Well, you do, sir. As you purport to speak for the town of Cantana, you may refuse," the man answered curtly, not smiling this time. "I feel that under the circumstances, I am being quite generous."

Pete leaned forward and offered his hand, slightly amused at this great man who was obviously accustomed to making deals and wielding power as some might brandish a sword. "I did not mean to make light of your generosity. I appreciate it, speaking for myself and the town," Pete said with a smile. The man released his firm grip and unfolded a legal document from his coat pocket. "Here is the agreement concerning my proposal. I have asked the president of the local bank with which we do business to witness the signing. I will give you a copy for your town and another will be registered here."

John escorted a tall man into the room, and he was introduced as the bank president. After the documents were signed and countersigned, Mr. Hill spoke with the man. "And Mr. Lawrence, I would like to emphasize that the railroad is very much interested in the town of Cantana and its welfare. You may pass that on to all the merchants and officials in town. It would disappoint me greatly to hear that these people were being put at a disadvantage by anyone."

The bank president nervously smoothed his mustache. "No sir, absolutely not. The situation will be monitored by me personally."

The banker quickly departed the train car as Mr. Hill turned to Pete.

"Marshal Randers, I have one more thing to give you.

Here is a letter from me, certifying that ten thousand dollars has been deposited in an account payable to the town of Cantana for civic improvements and maintenance as needed. I trust you will spend it honestly, wisely and well." With that, the man shook Pete's hand and wished him a good afternoon.

It was over, and Pete was in his buckboard, bumping along over the uneven prairie northeast of town. Cantana did not get its spur, but things seemed to have turned out perhaps for the best after all.

He was anxious to tell Alice all about it—that he, a common hayseed cowboy marshal, had just had dinner and done business with one of the greatest living Americans— but reality instantly set in as he remembered they were no longer friends.

16
ARLISS GOES FISHING

It was Thursday morning in late June, and Arliss had been collecting his freight orders from the various merchants in town all week. His freight business had nearly doubled since last autumn, and the storekeepers seemed happy to be receiving their goods on a consistent basis.

Arliss had rigged a second, smaller wagon to tow behind him, filling it each trip with coal and extra barrels of kerosene for the return trip to fulfill his idea of stocking up his warehouse with dry goods for the long winter ahead.

Bill Hester, the blacksmith and livery owner had asked him to buy him out so he could retire. Arliss cottoned to the idea with the thought that Hester's shop would be a perfect marriage to his freight business. Until Bill retired, Arliss would still drive the farrier's rig during the week, working around his trips to town, servicing the ranchers and farmers in the outlying areas.

Peedy would be going with him on this run to learn the business firsthand, and Arliss had promised to take him fishing if the weather was agreeable for a boy's camping trip.

Taking their time, Arliss and Peedy arrived in Havre on Saturday, and lodging the mules at the livery, they made their way to Mrs. Hays's restaurant for dinner. They took their seat at a corner table, and Mrs. Hays greeted them.

"Good afternoon, Sergeant Moore," she said with a smile. "And how is Peedy today?"

Peedy grinned. "You remembered my name, ma'am!"

"Well, how could I forget a young man with such a big appetite? What can I get you gentlemen today?"

"Could you make us up a nice picnic lunch?" Arliss requested. "Peedy and I are going fishing, and we thought we'd eat out by the water. Give us enough food for a dinner and supper, if you please. I brought this basket along to put things in."

"Oh, that sounds like such fun. How about fried chicken, some fried cornbread, baked beans, and an apple pie? Charlotte makes the best apple pie. You know Charlotte, don't you, Sergeant?" Mrs. Hays said with a coy smile.

Arliss smiled and folded his hands in front of him. "Yes, ma'am," he said with a subdued smile and pause. "I do."

Of course he knew Charlotte. He thought about her all the time, while he was shoeing horses, while he was driving his freight wagon across the prairie, while he lay his head on his pillow at night. Arliss stopped into Mrs. Hays's dining establishment to get supper every time he went to town whether he was hungry or not, just to look at her. He made a point of speaking to Charlotte when he could, and bringing her sweets or flowers. She was always cordial with him, acting as if she was happy to see him, but the fact that she'd soon be departing for Seattle always seemed to crop up somewhere in the conversation, a subtle reminder like a patch of ragweed on a hot August day.

"Charlotte is getting ready to leave work early today. I'll bet she would enjoy getting out of that hot kitchen for a picnic. Why don't you ask her?" Mrs. Hays asked.

Arliss did not smile or show any emotion. "Oh, Mrs. Hays. I don't think she'd have such a good time. Peedy and I are kind of rough hombres, and I have rented a buggy from the livery and plan to spend the afternoon with our hooks in the water, just the two of us."

Mrs. Hays turned to get their order. "You'll never know if you don't ask her," she said.

As Arliss and Peedy patiently waited for Mrs. Hays to fill their picnic basket with good things, Peedy squinted his eyes. "Mr. Arliss, who is Charlotte?" he asked.

"Charlotte is Mrs. Hays's cook," he said.

"Does Charlotte want to fish with us?" Peedy asked.

"I don't know, son. I didn't ask her," Arliss answered.

"Mr. Arliss, why don't you ask her to come with us? Maybe she'd like to fish."

"Boy, you're wearin' me out with your questions. Maybe she doesn't like to fish. If you want her to come with us so bad, why don't you ask her yourself?" Arliss said, confident that his challenge would end the matter. But before he could say any more, Peedy was up and like a shot, headed back to the kitchen.

"Son! Get back here!" Arliss shouted, but it was too late. Peedy had disappeared, and soon, the tall brown-skinned lady from Louisiana was walking out front with the boy leading her by the hand.

Standing there next to the table, she spoke. "Well, monsieur, we are meeting again. You send your son to ask me to the picnic?" Charlotte let loose of Peedy's hand and put her arm around him, drawing him close to her side, staring at Arliss as if she were waiting for him to explain.

Arliss spoke. "Mrs. Hays had this crazy notion that you might want to go fishing with us this afternoon. We have ordered a picnic supper to take along and have rented a buggy. I told Peedy that you might not want to go fishing, probably don't even know how."

"So, you think you know me, monsieur?" Charlotte said with a haughty smile. "I am from New Orleans—of course I know how to fish! Bring your buggy, monsieur, and I will go with you and your son Peedy, and perhaps I will teach you how we catch fish on the bayou."

* * *

A large stand of cottonwood trees grew along an oxbow bend in the Milk River north of town, shady, cool, and inviting. Charlotte and Peedy cleared off the ground beneath one huge tree, spreading a large white cloth to serve as their table for supper.

Peedy sat between Charlotte and Arliss as they fished, watching intently for a nibble, but all he got was a large dragonfly to perch on his bobber. Charlotte got a few tugs on her line, but Arliss quickly landed a nice channel catfish about twelve inches long, a prime eating size for this species of fish. Peedy caught nothing and was beginning to work himself up with disappointment.

"Calm down, son, and I'll tell you the best fishing story that ever happened to anyone since Jonah in the Bible. Do you want to hear?" Arliss said with a smile.

Holding his pole, Peedy nodded and listened intently. Arliss laid his pole down in the grass behind him and put his arm around Peedy's shoulder. "Well sir, when I was with the 10th United States Cavalry, the fightin'est unit in the whole army, I led a group of men on a patrol south of Fort Assiniboine, way past the Bear Paw Mountains. We had ridden all day and were dusty, tired, and hungry, almost too tired to break out our rations and make our coffee, beans, and bacon. Our scout found us a nice cool shady spot near a clear stream to make camp. Several of the men broke out their frying pans and the coffeepot, and we knew

145

that soon the beans would be simmering and the bacon crisp."

"Suddenly, the sky grew dark and the wind came up, and the clouds began to swirl like a big twister. We all ran to get the horses and find some cover next to a wall of jagged stone. The rain fell hard, filled with hail and falling straight to the ground. We covered our heads and faces after being struck again and again, and almost as soon as it started, the rain stopped and the clouds blew over, and before long we had the bright sun shining all around us. But do you know what else we saw?"

Arliss paused to look at Peedy, who sat with his eyes wide and mouth open. "My boys and I looked all around us, and there were fish—hundreds of fish flopping all over the place, in the grass, up on the rocks, and even some caught in the tree branches above us. We took off our hats and collected as many as we could and had the best doggone fish fry you ever saw. What do you think of that?"

Peedy could only shake his head.

"Well," Arliss went on. "One of the officers back at the fort had heard of the raining fish before; he even heard of it raining frogs and toads. He said that sometimes a twister will pass over a pond or lake and suck up all the fish and other critters and carry them many miles away and then dump them on the ground during a storm. That is what probably happened to us. There are no better tasting fish than those dropped from heaven!"

After Arliss's story, the Milk River seemed to come alive, and the fish started biting. Peedy did well, catching several bullheads and a two-pound channel catfish. Arliss held the boasting rights as he also caught a few catfish, one weighing at least fifteen pounds—until Charlotte changed all of that by hooking a massive fish that almost yanked the pole out of her hands. Taking a half-hour or more of tussle to best the monster, she pulled it out of the river with Arliss's help, surprised to see that it was a gray and white sturgeon stretching almost three feet with a long snout. It weighed nearly thirty pounds.

Looking at the huge fish wriggling in the grass beside the river, Arliss took his hat off and playfully bowed to Charlotte with an ear-to-ear grin. "You've beaten me. I've fished this river for years and have never seen one like it, never even heard of one. I take my hat off to you, Miss Charlotte Bossard Pénot of Louisiana."

Charlotte laughed and clapped her hands. "It was certainly just luck, big man. We could have had a wonderful fish fry with what we've caught today, yes?" she asked. "I have not had such a time before as today with my two new friends. Let us eat our picnic supper, Mr. Moore. Mrs. Hays has sent along a jug of sarsaparilla for us; it's cooling in the river."

After dishing up food for the big man and his adopted son, Charlotte leaned back and watched them eat. Chuckling out loud, she put her fingers over her mouth.

"Is something funny?" Arliss asked, munching on his chicken.

"I was just thinking, Mr. Moore, what mercy I have sent your way," she said, taking a bite out of her fried cornbread. "If not for Peedy here, I would have certainly made your chicken with the hot pepper sauce."

Arliss thought for a moment and then laughed. "I'm glad you didn't, but I think I could get used to that kind of cooking after a while." He looked into her eyes.

Charlotte blushed. "Ready for pie, Peedy?" she asked the boy, who seemed oblivious to the adults' conversation.

"I am making plans, Mr. Moore, to make my journey to Seattle before the first frost comes," Charlotte spoke with a sideways glance at Arliss.

"Mr. Arliss?" Peedy interrupted. "May I fish some more?"

"It's not polite for a young person to interrupt older folks when they're talking, son. Ask Miss Charlotte's pardon."

With contrition, Peedy stood up. "Sorry, Miss Charlotte," he said.

"Go along and fish, now," Arliss said firmly.

"Yes sir, Mr. Arliss," he responded, turning to find his pole and dig a few more worms under the leaves near the bank.

Charlotte grew quiet and then spoke. "Mr. Moore, how is it you call Peedy your son, but make him call you Mr.

Arliss? Is this not a contradiction, monsieur? If you have adopted him and call him your son, should he not call you father?"

Instead of showing irritation at Charlotte's subtle rebuke, Arliss reached over and took her hand. "This is what I'm talking about. I didn't know I was doing that. You did, and you've just helped me. I can't rear this boy into a man by myself." He paused. "He needs a mother too. Why don't you come help me?"

Gently pulling her hand back, she said, "What is it you are saying, monsieur—again with the boldness? I am on my way to Seattle to seek my fortune. This I have told you twice today, and many times before."

"If it is a fortune you seek, why not seek it here? I have started a freight business and may soon own my own blacksmith shop. Peedy needs a mother, and I need a wife. Why can't you stay here and help me do all of that?"

Charlotte rose to her feet. "I . . . I must go now." Turning on her heels, she quickly walked away, making her way along the riverbank and up over the tracks into town, soon disappearing from Arliss's sight.

Leaning back against the cottonwood tree thoughtfully, Arliss took a deep breath and sighed. He wished he had a fire and a long stick to poke it with.

She's right. My boldness frightened her away. I didn't think she was really that bent on going to Seattle. He shook his head and watched Peedy bait his hook. Standing up and walking

149

over to stand behind Peedy, he stooped down and put his hand on the young boy's shoulder.

"Peedy, would you do me a favor?" he asked with a tender smile. "From now on, would you just call me Pa?"

"Yes, sir," Peedy answered, putting his hand on Arliss's shoulder. "I would like to do that."

17
NOTHING IS EVER CONVENIENT

The letter Judith had left behind for Dan LaForge explained her reasons for returning east and her sorrow over Tom Brumett . . . but its open-ended wording was difficult to discern. Did he still have a chance with her? Was that her message in the veiled sentences he had read and reread many times in the last several months?

Seated at his desk at headquarters in Regina, Dan decided to take a chance and write her, asking her to accept his hand in marriage. He had been promoted to sergeant and would be reassigned to a post further north, a more stable life for a married couple than what he had now. Having received a special consideration for an outstanding record, Dan had been granted permission to marry. The rest was now in the hands of Judith Farnsworth.

He did not really expect her to return to Montana and meet him there, or even answer his letter, but he had to give her one last opportunity to say yes or no—by her words, her presence, or her silence.

Michael Leonard Jewell

* * *

Dan LaForge made his way across the southern portion of his jurisdiction, stopping at every small town along the way to make a presence, taking complaints and posting orders on the town message boards. He led an extra horse and pack mule behind him. Expecting to soon cross the border into Montana, he smiled, remembering the conversation he'd had with his inspector after filing his report.

"LaForge, I've read your report several times and commend you for a job well done. At least we've run down the rumors concerning these women, distilling it down to this one young girl you found. Now, saying that, there is this other matter. I took my compass and ruler and marked the distances between the nearest railroad depot in Canada and the nearest in Montana. No matter how I do it, the Canadian train seems to be a lot closer from where you found the girl. Can you explain to me why we took her to the United States and didn't just put her on our train to go back east?" The inspector had growled, handing Dan's report back to him.

Dan grasped the paper, looking up at his inspector, who was standing with his arms akimbo like a Dutch uncle. "Well, sir, this young girl was not well, and because the weather was bitter and the girl that frail, I didn't want to send her alone on the train without escort. Besides, I felt a need to investigate the matter further to be sure she did have family back east to take her in. I decided in my best judgment for her welfare to let her stay with some friends of mine close by in Montana. Friends who can be relied upon to see to her care, with a proper lawman nearby to watch over her safety, in a place where she can get her meals and a warm bed and a school she can attend. You know about my American friends in Montana, don't you, sir?"

The inspector looked over his glasses at Dan. "Yes, LaForge, I know all about your American friends in Montana! And the superintendent told me after reading this report of yours that if you spend any more time there, he's going to demand that the Americans start paying part of your salary. Now I don't mind you having friends across the border. It gets lonely out there sometimes, and between us, I did it myself. Just don't let it get out of hand."

That was four months ago, and now it was time to relieve Cantana of the responsibilities of caring for Ellen. He had brought an extra horse and a mule laden with adequate supplies for the return trip, but how this would all end up was still a mystery . . . and a bit of a quandary. Apparently, Ellen only had a few shirttail relations back east, and they were not willing or able to take responsibility for her. What he would finally do with Ellen to close the case at last would require the answers to several more questions.

Seeing Cantana in the distance, Dan glanced behind

him at the trailing horse and mule, assuring himself of their welfare. Making his way down Main Street in Cantana, he glanced down at his sleeve. He was not yet accustomed to seeing the bright yellow sergeant stripes recently sewn there—proof that he would be given more responsibility and authority. The new post further north would probably end his journeys to Montana for a long time, so he had prepared himself to say goodbye to his friends before returning home to Canada and a new assignment.

Stopping in front of Hester's, Dan led his horses and lone mule inside the stable, greeting and shaking the hand of the old blacksmith. As he walked up the steps to Granfield House, Ellen burst out of the doors, throwing her arms around his waist. "Corporal Dan! You're back," she shouted gleefully. "I didn't think you were ever going to come back."

Dan put his arm around her as they walked inside together. "I see that life in America suits you. Are you well, honey?" he asked, removing his gloves.

Ellen smiled. "I was silly to say those things. Alice and Mrs. Hamilton, my schoolteacher, have been so kind. I have had great fun with my new friends. It will be sad to say goodbye to them."

Dan was glad that Ellen had gotten along so well . . . and that she was expecting to return to Canada. This would make his job much easier, no matter how it went.

"Hello Danny," Alice said. "Sit down and have dinner

with Ellen. It will be ready in about a half-hour."

"Isn't the stage due in today?" he asked Alice. "I was expecting some mail."

"I look for it within the hour if it's on time. The coach driver is pretty good about timing his arrivals with the dinner bell," she laughed.

Dan and Ellen chatted away together at the table. She seemed genuinely glad to see him and went on about the last four months living in the small prairie town. He was almost sorry to take her away. After two years laboring as little more than a **skivvy** for the Norwegian innkeeper, she'd blossomed into a young girl again here. Cantana had allowed it.

After the server brought their food to the table, Dan spoke. "Ellen, I wasn't aware that there were so many things to do in the middle of the prairie. I don't think you could have been busier living in Regina."

Ellen took a bite of her codfish cake. "I helped make these, Dan," she said. "Alice and Isabelle have taught me so much about cooking. Try the fried potatoes and cottage cheese."

"This is very good, sweetie," he remarked as he sampled the fare. "I'm so happy that you had such a good time here."

"Dan? When are we going back to Canada, and what is going to happen to me?" she asked soberly.

As Sergeant LaForge sat back, he opened his mouth to

155

speak, but the rattle of the stagecoach broke the thread of his concentration. "Stay here, Ellen. I'll be right back," he said, rising from his chair and walking outside to the porch. There were several passengers disembarking this time, and as the last person stepped out onto the boardwalk, Dan smiled, put on his hat, and walked down the steps that way.

"Judith," he called out to the handsome young woman in a light blue dress. Walking up to her, Dan removed his Stetson hat and looked into her eyes.

"If I remember the last time we spoke, you were holding this," she said, reaching forward and placing her ungloved hand in his.

"May I kiss you?" Dan asked her, refusing to stand on ceremony.

Judith smiled and nodded once as the young Mountie held her and kissed her softly. "I did not think this would ever be possible, Judith. I think I'm dreaming," he said.

Judith smiled. "Are you sure you want to do this?" she asked. "You really don't know me."

"I do know you—better than you think," Dan answered. "And I do want this more than anything if you want it too."

Judith smiled. "Then let it be so. I thrive in the wilderness. Is Ellen here now?" Judith asked, putting her arm through his.

"She is inside and knows nothing of our plans. Let me break it to her. The final decision about her coming with us is hers," Dan answered, leading Judith inside to the table where Ellen was seated.

Ellen stood up as the couple approached. "Sit down honey," Dan said. "I want you to meet a very special lady — Judith Farnsworth."

* * *

Several days later on a bright sunny morning in Cantana, Sergeant Dan LaForge carefully readied the two horses and pack mule for the return trek northward to Canada. Helping Judith and Ellen onto the horse they would share, he turned to thank and wish his longtime friends well. Peggy Hamilton kissed Ellen and handed her a brown paper sack with freshly baked oatmeal cookies. Alice handed Dan a hamper of food to help ease the transition as they departed Cantana's meager civilization.

"Alice, this voucher from the Canadian government is for Ellen's board and is good as gold. Just redeem it at the bank in Havre," Dan instructed, giving Alice a farewell hug. "Tell Pete when you see him that I'm sorry I missed him. I will write you when I, or rather we, get settled. Perhaps someday I will be able to come back through. I wish you could come to our wedding, but it seems nothing is ever convenient, is it?"

"Danny?" Alice spoke with tears in her eyes, handing the voucher back to him. "We enjoyed having Ellen with us so much, and not for pay."

"Nonsense! You folks have a business here, not a charity. And Her Majesty settles her debts," Dan said with a smile. He mounted his horse, and with a wave, the three of them made their way up Main Street to the yellow grasses north of town.

18

GIVEN ONE MORE CHANCE

Conscious of the need to spend time with young Peedy, Arliss tried to take him along on his journeys whenever he could—when he was not in school, that is. Starting out one morning in August as the sun stood on its feet along the eastern horizon, Arliss and Peedy headed west in the farrier's rig to a ranch about twenty miles away to spend the day, or however long, caring for the shoeing, grooming, and ailments of the rancher's equine stock. It was a large spread, and having already established a good reputation with the rancher and foreman, Arliss was treated well. On such visits he often picked up incidental work mending tools, leather, and other things requiring the skills of an expert blacksmith.

Peedy liked to visit this particular ranch because the cowboys were especially kind to him, letting him hang around and watch the activity in the big corral, especially breaking in the new horses. When the cook rang the triangular dinner bell signaling it was time to eat, one of the cowboys would almost certainly scoop him up and set him

159

down beside him at the table. Peedy could not decide if he wanted to be a cowboy or a farrier, or perhaps when he was older, he would get to drive a freight wagon of his own. Now he was too little and too young, but one day soon his time would come.

As the late afternoon of the second day came upon them, Arliss loaded up his rig, and with Peedy beside him all tuckered out, they set out for home, prepared to make camp on the prairie later that evening.

About an hour out from the ranch, Arliss drove his rig along the ridge of a deep coulee, pulling the reins abruptly to stop the mules. Letting his eyes focus in the ever-increasing dusk, he was startled at what he saw. In the muddy floor of the coulee were about two dozen buffalo in a wallow, seemingly oblivious of their presence.

Carefully waking Peedy, who had fallen asleep on the seat beside him, he pointed out the creatures. They were both in awe, and Arliss grew sober as he realized that he might be looking at the last buffalo alive in the wilds of Montana—maybe even the world. Carefully turning the rig around and heading back to the ranch, Arliss asked, "Peedy, son, have you ever seen a buffalo before?"

"No, sir. I heard about them, but someone said they were all dead forever," Peedy responded while rubbing his sleepy eyes.

"Well, there was a time, not that long ago, that millions and millions of buffalo were spread out all across the Great

Plains. They were the Indians' cattle but were hunted and killed so much that almost all of them are gone. A few ranchers that care about the buffalo have taken them in and are protecting them. Mr. Lloyd, the owner of the ranch where we spent the day, is one of those ranchers. He has a small herd of them he keeps fenced in for their protection, and I'll bet he would like to send his cowboys out and herd those few buffalo back there to his ranch for safety. If someone doesn't help them, they will be hunted and wiped out completely. We need to tell him about them and give those big fellows one more chance to make it."

* * *

Several days later, back in Cantana, Arliss made ready to make another run to the Hi-line for supplies. It had rained all night, and he was sure the trail to Havre would be a muddy one. Thumbing through the merchant's orders once more, he set out in the dark across the prairie in the large lumber wagon he had rebuilt to haul freight with the smaller coal wagon in tow behind. Arliss had since added two more mules to his team of four to help carry the extra weight of the coal wagon. He expected his speed to be slower due to the soft muddy ground, and he didn't much care. He had something on his mind, and he needed all the extra time to think it through.

The rain was coming down harder now, borne by a

161

brisk gusty wind out of the north. Since he was headed southwest, the direction of his travel helped keep the torrent to his back and out of his face. He was glad that Peedy was safe and warm back home in Cantana. They had spoken often the last few days about the small herd of buffalo they had seen several days ago while on the job at Mr. Lloyd's ranch. Arliss was pleased to know there were now thirty-two more of these magnificent creatures safely inside the fences on the ranch due to Mr. Lloyd's love for these great animals.

Getting into town the next day, he lodged his mules, parking his wagons beside the livery. Arliss was hungry, and as he set out for Mrs. Hays's place, he was taken aback by his own disheveled appearance staring back at him in the tall store glass window.

Nothing I can do about it now. I've been riding in the rain for a day and a half, and after unharnessing six muddy mules, I'm certainly a sight. He took an inconspicuous seat in the corner of the dining area. To his surprise, he was waited on by a new girl, who took his order of steak and eggs.

"Is Charlotte not working today?" he asked the waitress.

"She is doing the cooking now, but she will be leaving this evening on the train for Seattle," the girl said.

Arliss said nothing but finished his meal, expecting or hoping to see Charlotte peeking out at him from the kitchen door. But finally, shrugging his big shoulders, he stood up and placed a silver dollar and a fifty-cent piece next to his plate. Time to go.

He made his way to the door. But as he reached to grasp the door handle, he suddenly turned and quickly made his way back to the kitchen.

Arliss could feel the steamy heat hit him as he walked through the doorway. Charlotte was cooking alone, frying meat in a cast-iron pan on the large iron stove, dripping with perspiration. Startled to see someone walk into her kitchen, she quickly turned to see who was there.

"Charlotte?" Arliss said. "Sorry for running you off that day we went fishing, but I've decided to take one more crack at it, to give you one more chance in case my intentions were not clear. I'm declaring for you, Charlotte. I need you, and Peedy needs you. I could profess my love, but you probably wouldn't believe me. If love and good fortune means worship and money and buying you everything you could ever want, then I fall down flat. If it means a place to call home, and a man and a son to love you, then maybe that's what you're really looking for and you just don't know it."

Arliss pressed his hat on his head. "I'm getting ready to harness up the mules and load up my wagons for the drive back to Cantana. If what I've been talking about is something you might want, I'll be driving past the train station on my way out of town. If I see you standing there, you can come along with me and we can get married in

163

Cantana. But if not, I'll understand."

Arliss nodded once and pinched the brim of his hat as he left Mrs. Hays's establishment.

Charlotte continued to cook the orders she had been given by the waitress. Mrs. Hays would take over for her in about an hour, and then her job would be done. Her bags were already packed, and she was due to take the evening train west. Everything in her young life had already been settled, and that was that.

Pretty and self-assured, Charlotte knew who she was and what she wanted to do. But now she was flustered, wrestling with feelings she couldn't explain and wasn't prepared to deal with. She was being offered another kind of life very different from the one she had imagined for herself in Seattle.

Oh, why did that blessed man have to cross my path? she thought, slamming the heavy iron lid down on the smoking pot before her.

19
PETE GETS AN OFFER

Pete stood in the doorway of his office thoughtfully sipping from his cup, gazing out at the steady drizzle that had been falling all that morning. *Coffee sure tastes good on a day like this,* he thought, remembering the pleasant camaraderie he'd had with his father and the joy he had felt as a boy camping out in the wilds of Minnesota. Fried fish never tasted better than they did back then, and the biscuits his father made by rolling out dough into long snakes and twisting them around a green stick, baking them to golden brown over a gentle bed of glowing coals, were heaven.

Pa has sure been gone for a long time, he thought. He missed him terribly as he fixed his eyes across the street at Granfield House, wondering what Alice might be doing now, missing their chats and the way she would playfully feed him when they had breakfast together. He missed her love and the attention he'd thought he could always count on, the love he'd believed would always be there.

"Excuse me, Marshal," said a tall cavalry sergeant on a

horse that had slipped up beside him unawares, breaking his concentration. "Didn't mean to startle you, sir, but I'm trying to get some information. My patrol and I are trying to locate a man wanted by the army for murder. We received information from an Indian scout that a white man was seen around an alkali lake near here. Have you heard of it?"

"Yes," Pete answered, pointing over his shoulder. "Its several miles due east of here. Want me to show you?"

"I would be much obliged, Marshal. My men are waiting for me just outside of town. This man we are seeking is a pretty cool customer, wanted for killing several Indians south of the fort. He will stick at nothing if he is cornered. We need to get him before he slips away into Canada." Pete mounted his horse and followed the sergeant to his men.

About two hours later, they had arrived at the area. Pete spoke to the sergeant. "This place is sort of a collection of small lakes created by old meanders. There are lots of places to hide. If this fellow you're after sees us, he'll hightail it north across the border. Can I suggest something?"

"Go ahead," the sergeant answered.

"Let's break up in pairs and spread ourselves out. If we can get far enough out in front of him, we will be able to see him from several angles when he moves."

"Men?" the sergeant shouted. "Do as the marshal says.

Every one of you find his partner and spread out. If you locate Mr. Watkins, approach him as quietly as you can, but if he sees you, fire a couple of warning shots in the air to let the rest of us know where you are. Follow him and wear him down, but if he turns north to Canada . . . you know what you have to do. Try to take him alive, but we can't let him get away. He'll just kill again if we do. Now move out!"

The troopers quickly headed out, doing their best to quickly infiltrate this strange landscape of rutted meander scars and oxbow lakes, all intent on flushing out this man Watkins, who had proven that killing came easy to him.

Pete had paired up with the sergeant. He expected a long, weary day ahead, but in less than an hour, several shots rang out more than a mile in the distance near the border—then a pause and several more shots. Hurrying that way, Pete and the sergeant arrived on the scene to find Watkins lying face down near the shore of a small lake.

"He spotted us, Sarge, and fired," a nervous young trooper muttered. "He . . . he gave us no choice."

The sergeant said nothing as he gazed at the silent form lying in their midst. "Well, lay him over his horse and let's get headed back. Cover him with a blanket and tie him up good. Don't want any kids or the ladies to have to see this."

Pete had witnessed this scenario a few times in his earlier days, shadowing his father, who had been a scout for the army years ago. There always seemed to be men who just refused to surrender, or figuring they would get

167

the rope anyhow, chose to flee and fight it out, giving the soldiers or lawmen no choice on what to do.

Pete watched as the sergeant dismounted and examined the body, turning it over to observe a single bullet hole through the man's upper chest. It would have been better if there were more bullet holes, to leave it a mystery as to whose bullet actually did the killing. But there it was—one .30 caliber slug hole from an army Krag rifle.

Turning around, the sergeant looked at the pair of young troopers who had been compelled to answer Watkins's murderous gunfire in kind. Quick inspection of the first man's rifle made it obvious that it had not been fired. Taking the second man's rifle, he opened the breech and the cover of the magazine; there were only two unfired cartridges left. The magazine normally held five.

As the old sergeant held the rifle in his right hand, he approached the trooper, who was probably not yet twenty-one years old. Putting his hand on the young man's shoulder, he walked him a few yards in the distance away from the rest of the men. The old sergeant looked into his eyes and spoke several words as the boy nodded. Patting the young man's back, he handed him his rifle and walked away, giving the young trooper time to deal with having taken a life for the first time. Pete did not know what the sergeant had said, but the words were obviously meant to be comforting.

* * *

The stage rattled down Main Street, stirring up the dust. The driver paused for several moments before opening the doors to allow the air to clear. Pete met the driver and grasped the mailbag, tucking it under his arm and taking hold of a stack of packages going to Granfield House.

Following the single passenger who had disembarked the stage on his way to the hotel, Pete put the packages on the counter and handed Alice the mailbag without so much as a mutual greeting or eye contact. He waited for the sorting to be done. Tossing him a letter across the counter, Alice turned to walk away, disappearing in the back room that served as the hotel office.

A wounded spirit who can bear? Pete thought, quoting the verse from Proverbs in his head as he watched Alice turn to leave. But he was just as guilty of this as she.

Pete shrugged and abruptly left the hotel in a huff, bounding off the top step of the porch to return to his dreary office. Stopping at his small stove, he ladled a bowl of reheated stew for his dinner and grabbed a cold biscuit from that morning's breakfast. It had been Pete's custom to eat his meals at Granfield House, a perk allowed him as marshal of the town. But he had not eaten there since his fallout with Alice, instead carrying on as usual, batching it and making his own meals as he'd done when he was a deputy for Marshal Brenton.

Sopping up some gravy with his biscuit and taking a few bites, he opened the envelope he had received in the mail. It was addressed to him personally, and was from the army at Fort Assiniboine. Quickly scanning the lines, he read the words of gratitude, thanking him for his assistance in the capture of the outlaw Watkins. "Huh!" he grunted in surprise. "Imagine that."

The short letter of thanks also contained in its postscript a request for Pete to come to Fort Assiniboine at his convenience and speak with the army about accepting a position as army scout. Since so many soldiers had been sent off to Cuba and the Philippines, there was a shortage of good scouts. The pay was good, better than he was getting now, and Pete was qualified, having been taught well by his father.

Washing his bowl and spoon in the water bucket next to the stove, he set them on a shelf by the wall to air-dry. Then walking across the room to the window, he stood gazing out to the hotel.

It's been kind of tough seeing Alice go about her business day after day like she doesn't need me anymore, he thought.

Sitting down again at his desk, he quickly dashed off a letter and stuffed it in an envelope, then hurried across Main Street to the hotel, handing the letter to the departing stagecoach driver. Pete turned and walked away to make his usual rounds about town. *They should be able to get along fine without me now that Ben's here*, Pete thought.

* * *

Peggy Hamilton closed and locked the door to the schoolhouse and walked in the direction of her home, but thinking better of it, she briskly turned and walked up the boardwalk to Granfield House instead.

"Do you have time for a cup of tea?" Peggy asked Alice, who was seated at her desk in her office.

Looking up quickly as if she had been drawn back from somewhere else, Alice smiled. "Yes, I do, and Isabelle just made a batch of cinnamon rolls. Find us a table in the dining room and I'll get us some." She removed her spectacles and tossed her pencil on the desk.

Peggy and Alice chatted for a half-hour or more about generalities including the school, the hotel, and Ben . . . but Peggy thought it curious that Pete was never mentioned. She knew that Alice and Pete had fallen out but was surprised that after all this time the rift had not been mended. Taking a chance, she decided to confront Alice.

"Alice? May I speak to you about something personal?" she asked, setting down her cup of tea.

Pressing her lips together, Alice answered, "If you can't who can, Peg?"

"Are you and Pete still having a spat? We've been talking for over a half-hour, and you have not mentioned him once. Pete is supposed to be the love of your life. What

171

happened?"

Taking a deep breath with a sigh, Alice looked into Peggy's eyes. "We haven't spoken three words since Pete left that day to go find Ben and Arliss. You were there and heard it. I was pretty upset. Pete stormed out, and neither one of us is willing to get past our hurt feelings to make it up. He feels wronged and thinks that when I questioned his judgment, I went too far and crossed a line. I don't know how to fix it, Peg." Alice's eyes sparkled with moisture.

Peggy sat quietly for a moment, allowing Alice time for composure. "Ben told me that Pete hardly says a word anymore unless it directly involves the job, and he refuses to say what's ailing him. I know that when it comes to hurt feelings, nothing seems to make sense, but Alice, if you let this thing fester too long, it won't matter anymore. One or both of you will go your own way. Waiting for the other person to make the first move sometimes means that nobody does anything. Take it from an old married girl. You two need to end this, or the damage won't be undone."

* * *

Deputy Marshal Ben Hamilton walked up the steps to Granfield House, opening the French doors and walking in. Alice was seated in the back corner with a stack of papers strewn across the table where she was working.

"Good morning, Alice. Letting you know that if you

need any help from the marshal, I'll be minding the store until Pete gets back."

Alice seemed mildly surprised. "Oh, is Marshal Randers not here?"

Ben sighed. *Marshal Randers indeed!* "Yes, he left early this morning for Fort Assiniboine."

"Oh," Alice said, looking up. "Is he escorting a prisoner?"

"No, the army wants to hire him as a scout. I guess he impressed them when he helped them find that murderer awhile back. That's all I know." Ben waved and smiled, exiting the hotel to make his rounds.

Alice put down her pencil, which rolled across the table and fell to the floor. She looked about the almost empty dining room.

"I've lost him," she muttered under her breath.

20
AFTER A LONG WINTER

The winter had been long and harsh, but the citizens of Cantana were kept warm and well supplied due to Arliss's idea of building up an inventory of dry goods and other commodities such as kerosene and coal in his warehouse. In the past, vendors had taken advantage of Cantana's remoteness, lack of good roads, and comparatively small orders by gouging the townsfolk with inflated prices, knowing they were helpless to protest. But Arliss had been able to circumvent this by making a way for Cantana to supply itself, giving the ranchers and dirt farmers in the area another option. And by the time the warm April breezes blew through town, Arliss had successfully completed his third freight run of the year to Havre.

Charlotte had weathered the bitter prairie winter, wondering from time to time what would have happened had she left that day on the train for Seattle. She had never envisioned herself as a wife or a mother, not having observed many examples of happy couples over the years. But the Methodist preacher on his monthly circuit had married them, and now Arliss had a wife, Peedy had a mother, and Charlotte had a partner who was well able to match her strength and sass.

Charlotte was not sure at first if she loved Arliss, but what was love really but a commitment to someone, to care for them, be a companion, helper, and true partner? *Maybe the sparks and emotional part of love will come later,* she'd thought last autumn when she climbed aboard the freight wagon and agreed to accompany Arliss back to Cantana and be his wife.

Charlotte blushed and smiled when she thought about that day. The sparks had indeed come!

* * *

The first stage to arrive in Cantana after the particularly long and brutal winter slammed to a sudden halt in front of Granfield House, as it would do every two weeks for the foreseeable future. Citizens of this isolated prairie town were dependent upon the stagecoach for such luxuries as regular mail service and a sure way back to civilization. But as a rule, folks didn't often come to Cantana to take up residence, making passengers a great curiosity and a gazingstock to the town's citizens. Such was the case today.

"Whoa!" the driver shouted as he stood up straight on the brake lever, waiting for the dust to plume away in the wind. There was a lone passenger aboard this time, and not waiting for assistance, he opened the door himself and confidently stepped up onto the boardwalk, his heavy outer coat draped over his arm. Well turned-out in a black, double-breasted Prince Albert frock coat, he looking about him to get his bearings and spoke to the driver to have his trunk and baggage removed to the hotel.

Signing in at the clerk's desk, the man said nothing but made his way to the dining room and took a seat. Alice peeked around the corner at him along with several other citizens taking their meals at Granfield House. Nonchalantly, the tall, thin man, over six feet with a short, well-groomed beard and mustache, removed his hat and laid it with his coat and stick across the chair next to him at his table. He exuded the air of a professional man. Alice noticed his habit of nervously removing his round wire-rimmed glasses several times to polish the lenses as he waited for someone to serve him.

Concentrating on his meal of roast chicken, mashed potatoes, and fried parsnips, the stranger pulled a newspaper from his coat pocket and casually scanned the front page, holding it in his left hand and his fork in the other.

"No dessert, thank you," he said to the waitress. "But I will have another cup of tea. Very good tea you have here. You must have good water." The man did not make eye contact when he spoke, as if he could have been speaking to anybody.

Finally, standing to leave, he gathered his things . . . but before finding his room, he stopped at the clerk's desk to speak with Alice.

"Young lady," he began, "I see there are many empty buildings in town. Is there someone in particular I can speak to about them? I might be interested in purchasing one if they are for sale."

Alice was mildly surprised. "Marshal Randers would be the best person to speak with, but he won't be back in town until tomorrow," she answered.

"That will be fine. I am not going anywhere," the man said with a slight bow. "May I have a bath in my room? Thank you." With that, he turned and walked up the long staircase.

Alice watched him disappear from view and then spun the guest register around, examining closely what the stranger had written when he signed in.

R. Whitaker, she read, wondering who the man could be who wanted to purchase property in a town where the ghosts outnumbered the living.

21
THE NEW BADGE

It was dark and the sun long set. Pete was weary and had fallen asleep once or twice in his saddle as he made his way across the lonely prairie, searching the eastern horizon for any lamplight that would tell him he was nearing the town of Cantana and home. Stopping to take a drink from his canteen, he struck a match to gaze upon the dial of the old army compass his father had given him, to make certain that he had not in his weariness ridden past town.

But Pete smiled when his horse, seeming to have a keener sense of direction than its weary rider, adjusted to the northeast. Soon he was riding down Main Street in Cantana. Taking his horse to Hester's for feed and water and much needed rest, Pete pulled his rifle from the saddle and threw his war bags over his shoulder, walking across the street to his office. Ben had just returned from his last round about the town.

"Go on home to Peggy, Ben," Pete said. "I'll see ya in the morning." Ben put on his hat but lingered for a few moments, waiting for Pete to tell him what he didn't want to hear—that he had accepted the position as army scout.

Pete said nothing but hung up his hat and holster, pouring out the last dregs of old coffee from the pot and refilling it with fresh water for morning. "Anything I need to know, Ben?" Pete asked.

"It's been pretty quiet, Pete," Ben answered with his hand on the doorknob. "The saloon is almost empty. I guess I'll see you in the morning."

When the door closed, Pete sat down at his desk, and leaning back in his chair, closed his eyes. He was hungry but too tired to heat up a pan. *I could go down to Macgregor's,* he thought, suddenly overcome with a hankering for fried chicken. It was so strong he could smell it.

Then it hit him: that *was* fried chicken he was smelling.

Pete opened his eyes again and was startled to see Alice standing beside him and a tray of hot food covered with a towel on the desk in front of him. "Alice?" he said.

She smiled. "Oh, you poor thing. How tired you look." She brushed his hair back with her hand and pulled up a chair beside him. "Here, I brought you some fried chicken, fried potatoes, and cottage cheese. And yes; that is apple pie there beside it."

Pete looked at Alice, not knowing what to say. "Am I dreaming? What just happened?" Alice leaned forward and kissed him softly on his unshaven cheek. "I love you, Peter. I didn't mean to upset you or tell you how to do your job. I was just afraid you were going to get killed, that's all. I'm so sorry. If there's any chance of fixing this, I would like for us to go on the way things were." She laid her head against his shoulder and asked, "Is that yet possible?"

Pete rubbed his eyes and put his arm around her. "I'm sorry too, that I let this thing go on for so long. I have a stubborn streak inherited from my pa. I've never wanted anything more than to marry you."

Alice said nothing but removed the towel from the tray and tucked it around Pete's neck. She then scooped up a spoonful of fried potatoes and fed them to Pete, wiping his mouth with the corner of the towel and kissing him softly in the glow of the lamp that rested on the corner of his desk.

* * *

That day, the sun lost its power to penetrate the heavy gray clouds that had settled over the Montana prairie. There was no rain, but coolness rested over the town as folks gathered at the Hamilton's house for a small celebration put together for Ben Hamilton, to honor him and welcome him back safely to his job as deputy marshal of Cantana.

The house was crowded, and the ladies had set up a sort of buffet so everyone could dish up their own plates. Several roasted chickens, golden brown, sat on the narrow counter waiting to be carved. Mashed potatoes, gravy, pickled beets, sourdough bread, and carrots roasted with butter and brown sugar rounded out the meal. And after a prayer to God for thanks, they ate the supper heartily, happy to be in each other's company.

Then it was time for coffee and cake. As Alice cut the long sheet cake into squares, Pete stood up and asked for everyone's attention.

"Folks? I have something here for Ben," he said, taking something from his pocket and holding it up high for all to see. "Now Ben, this is your old badge, the badge that we found nailed to the office door. I want to keep it in my desk as a remembrance of the Lord's goodness, for keeping you safe and bringing you back to us." Pete held the badge up high for all to gaze upon one last time, its shape somewhat distorted by the large spike hole that had been thrust through its heart.

"Peggy, I'm going to ask you to come over here next to Ben."

Peggy made her way over and sat next to her husband, holding his hand with teary eyes.

"Ben, I want you to know that you made us all proud, but a deputy can't go around with a hole in his badge." Reaching in his pocket, Pete pulled out a small wooden box and handed it to Peggy with a wide smile. "Peg, if you will present this to your husband, I would be most grateful."

Peggy opened the box, and there inside was a shiny new deputy's badge with the words *Ben Hamilton, Chief Deputy Marshal* engraved on the back. Peggy handed the badge to her husband, who fumbled to pin it on his shirt.

"Thanks, Pete," Ben said. "But this is a heck of way to go about getting a new badge. And what is the difference between a deputy and a chief deputy?"

Pete paused for a moment. "Well, I suppose it means that if I ever hire more deputies, you get to boss them around, but for now, it means more responsibility for the same amount of pay." There was a wave of laughter from those in the room, glad that there could be some joy associated with the grim story concerning Ben's badge.

Pete held his hand up again. "Folks, folks, I have something else I'd like to say. One of our newest citizens to Cantana, who came here to live just a short time ago, has changed our town in many ways for the better. His freight business has made it possible for us to cut ourselves loose from the bloodsuckers that would let us freeze and starve. It was his bravery and competence that saved my life and the life of Ben Hamilton. I speak, of course, of my best friend Arliss Moore, the old buffalo soldier of the 10th U.S. Cavalry. Arliss, would you stand up, please?"

Arliss slowly rose to his feet. It was obvious he had not expected this, and as the tough old cavalry soldier displayed his true meekness, it was evident that he possessed a great depth of character.

Pete continued. "I had no idea what to do for Arliss, to show him how we felt about him, so this is what I came up with. Charlotte? Would you present this to your husband?"

Pete handed her a small wooden box, similar to the one given Ben. Sliding open the lid, she uncovered a gold badge with the words *Special Deputy* embossed on the front. With tears in her eyes, Charlotte handed the badge to Arliss, surprised and touched by the genuine feelings the people held for her husband. Arliss looked at the badge and turned it over. His name and the words *Buffalo Soldier* were engraved on the back. Arliss said nothing but smiled and nodded, holding the badge in his hand.

Pete looked at his friend. "Arliss, since you have continued to resist being deputized, I thought you might accept the position of special deputy, to be kept in reserve and called upon by the town when needed." It was obvious that Arliss was uncomfortable with all the attention, so Alice spoke. "There is plenty of food, folks. Either you eat it up now, or I will force you to take some home with you as leftovers."

As the tenor of the moment changed, Alice grinned. *Menfolk can be too serious if you let them.*

* * *

"Mr. Whitaker, I am presuming," Pete said, standing behind his desk to greet the man who had just walked into his office.

"Yes sir, you have presumed correctly. And I believe I am correct that you are Marshal Randers?" The men shook hands. "Miss Granfield said you might be able to direct me concerning certain properties in the town? I may be interested in putting out my shingle here in Cantana. What an unusual name for a town, is it not?"

Pete smiled. "Yes sir. Someone long ago thought it would be clever to combine Canada and Montana to be our name since we are so close to the border. After you have lived here for a while, though, the humor of it escapes you. May I offer you some coffee?"

"I just came from breakfast, Marshal. Thank you," Whitaker said. "Since you seem to be most familiar with the buildings in town, I am looking for a place near the hotel. I am prepared to redecorate and refurbish at my own expense if the price is acceptable. I am more accustomed to the hustle and bustle of a metropolitan area—I am from Chicago, you know. But I am now looking for a slower pace, somewhere I am truly needed. My niece suggested this place in the wilderness. 'Nice people there,' she told me."

Pete stared at the man, who stood blinking at him through his round glasses. "Mr. Whitaker, may I ask you what your business is? That might help me to find what you are looking for."

"Actually, Marshal, it's Doctor Whitaker. I am a doctor of medicine and have retired from my practice in Chicago. My health requires that I lessen my pace, so my niece suggested Cantana."

Pete was surprised and thrilled at the same moment.

The very thing Cantana had need of! "Sir, may I ask the name of your niece?"

"You may know her already—Judith Farnsworth. Her aunt is my sister. Judith and my sister were very encouraging and said it would be a fine thing if I would come and be your doctor."

Bless her heart for thinking of us, Pete thought. "Well, Doctor," Pete began, "it just happens that the old doctor's office is available. Let me show it to you."

"That would be fine. I have always wanted to visit the West and the frontier. I have always enjoyed and been inspired by the writings of Theodore Roosevelt, and when Judith told me about this place and her adventures with the Indians and her parents as missionaries, I decided to take a chance."

Pete led him across the street to show him the dusty, dark remnants of old Doc Blake's office. He unlocked the weathered door and brushed back the cobwebs. The room had not been bothered since that day several years ago when he and Tom Brumett foraged through the old doctor's things to locate medicines and instruments to take with them to the Bear Paw Mountains.

Doctor Whitaker seemed to be enchanted by what he saw, and by the thought that he, a modern university trained medico from Chicago, might have his taste of the Old West in his golden years.

"I must have this place, Marshal," he said. "What is the

price?"

"Well, Doctor Whitaker," Pete said with a grin, "today is a good day for a doctor to purchase an office here in town. Old Doc Blake left instructions when he passed that this office was to be sold to the next doctor willing to set up shop here in Cantana for the sum of one dollar, and if the new doc couldn't afford it, he left a silver dollar in his desk drawer to pay for it himself."

Doctor Whitaker could not help but laugh, and he handed Pete a shiny Morgan silver dollar. "I'll get my receipt from you later, Marshal." Whitaker said as he looked about him. "This place will stand some work. There must be an inch of dust on everything. Could you advise me of any resident carpenters in town whom I might hire to begin putting this place back into working order?"

But before Pete could speak, he was interrupted by heavy footfalls outside on the boardwalk. It was Deputy Ben Hamilton, running in the direction of Granfield House.

"Ben? What's wrong?" Pete shouted.

"Pete, I need to get Alice. It's Peggy. The baby is coming!" Turning to Doctor Whitaker, Pete spoke. "Well Doc, I think we have your first customer. The Hamilton's new baby is hankering to

be born. If you'll follow Ben back to his place, I'll get your instrument bag from your room at Granfield House."

The End

CPSIA information can be obtained
at www.ICGtesting.com
Printed in the USA
FFOW03n0513060618
47023182-49301FF